WENDY MASS & REBECCA STEAD

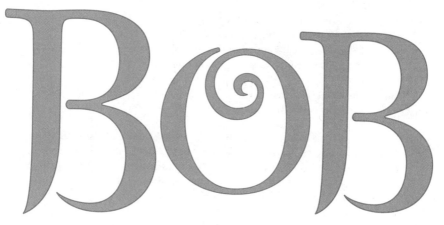

with illustrations by
NICHOLAS GANNON

SQUARE
FISH

FEIWEL AND FRIENDS
NEW YORK

SQUARE
FISH

An imprint of Macmillan Publishing Group, LLC
175 Fifth Avenue, New York, NY 10010
mackids.com

Our books may be purchased in bulk for promotional, educational,
or business use. Please contact your local bookseller or the Macmillan
Corporate and Premium Sales Department at (800) 221-7945 ext. 5442
or by email at MacmillanSpecialMarkets@macmillan.com.

Library of Congress Cataloging-in-Publication Data
Names: Mass, Wendy, 1967– author. | Stead, Rebecca, author. | Gannon,
  Nicholas, illustrator.
Title: Bob / Wendy Mass and Rebecca Stead ; illustrated by Nicholas Gannon.
Description: New York : Feiwel and Friends, 2018. | Summary: Visiting her
  grandmother in Australia, Livy, ten, is reminded of the promise she made
  five years before to Bob, a strange, green creature who cannot recall who
  or what he is.
Identifiers: LCCN 2017041215| ISBN 978-1-250-30869-6 (paperback) |
  ISBN 978-1-250-16663-0 (ebook)
Subjects: | CYAC: Imaginary creatures—Fiction. | Memory—Fiction. |
  Lost children—Fiction. | Grandmothers—Fiction. | Australia—Fiction.
Classification: LCC PZ7.M42355 Bob 2018 | DDC [Fic]—dc23
LC record available at https://lccn.loc.gov/2017041215

Originally published in the United States by Feiwel and Friends
First Square Fish edition, 2019
Book designed by April Ward
Square Fish logo designed by Filomena Tuosto

5   7   9   10   8   6

AR: 3.9 / LEXILE: 590L

For mysterious creatures everywhere

CHAPTER ONE

LIVY

I feel bad that I can't remember anything about Gran Nicholas's house. On the table in her kitchen Gran has lined up three things I do not remember:

1. A green stuffed elephant in overalls.

2. A net bag full of black chess pieces.

3. A clunky old tape recorder.

"You loved these things when you were here before," Gran Nicholas tells me.

But I don't remember any of it.

"Not the horses?" Gran Nicholas says, pointing out the window to a dusty yard. Maybe there were horses there once?

"Not the pigs?" Gran Nicholas says, pointing out the back door. If I squint I can make out some pigs behind a fence. But I don't remember them.

"Not *this*?" she says, holding up the green stuffed elephant. "When you were here before, you wouldn't let go of it. You carried it everywhere. You wouldn't let anyone get near it!"

But it's like I've never laid eyes on that green stuffed elephant in my life. It could have been anyone's green stuffed elephant, and I would not have minded.

Mom looks nervous. She wants me to remember. But it's her fault I don't—she brought me here for a month when I was five and didn't bring me back again until now, when I am practically eleven.

Ten and a half.

Almost.

Of course, I do remember Gran herself, because we talk on the phone every week, and we write each other postcards. Gran tells me the news of Australia and I tell her the news of Massachusetts. She came to visit us once, for two weeks. But I don't remember one thing about her house.

Actually, maybe I *do* remember one thing.

I think I remember a wrong chicken.

I remember chickens, and one chicken that was different. One chicken was not like the other chickens, is what I remember. But standing here in the kitchen with everyone looking at me, I don't know how to ask Gran about that.

I pick up the elephant. It's soft and floppy. I still don't remember it.

Gran Nicholas sighs. She doesn't say what I know she wants to say, which is that we should have come back sooner.

On the other hand, Australia is very far away from Massachusetts.

If you want to get from our house to Gran Nicholas's house, this is what you have to do:

1. Drive from Massachusetts to New York City for four hours.

2. Park the car and wait for a bus to the airport.

3. Take a plane for seven hours to California.

4. Get off that plane.

5. Take another plane for nineteen hours to Melbourne, Australia.

6. Get off that plane.

7. Wait in three different lines while official people look at your bags and your papers.

8. Wait in the rental car line.

9. Drive the car for two hours in Australia.

10. Get to Gran's house.

Now Mom's going to leave me here again while she goes to visit all her friends from growing up. The baby is too young to stay with Gran Nicholas, so she's going with Mom.

I wonder what it's like here at night.

I look at the chess pieces. Does Gran have the white ones? I open my mouth to ask, but instead I hear myself say:

"Are there . . . chickens?"

"Yes!" She gets excited, and Mom looks happy. Gran grabs my hand and runs me out to the yard, where some chickens are pecking in the dirt. I look them over but they all look regular.

"Are these the same chickens?" I ask Gran Nicholas.

She says they are different chickens. But the *idea* of chickens is right.

I don't exactly know how to ask the next question. "Did you used to have one that was . . . weird?"

"Weird?" she asks.

Maybe there wasn't a weird one. Or maybe they don't say *weird* in Australia.

"Never mind," I say. I realize I'm squeezing something in the hand that Gran is not holding. I open it and see one of the black chess pieces. A pawn.

Then, coming back into the house with Gran, I see Gran's back stairs. They have carpet on them, and I suddenly know that I have bumped down those stairs.

"Did I ever bump down those stairs?" I ask Gran, pointing.

"Yes!" she says. "You loved bumping down those stairs. You had a name for it."

"A name for the stairs?"

"No, for bumping down them. You called it something. . . ."

I think she is right. I think I did call it something. But neither of us can remember what it was.

Now that I've remembered the chickens and the stairs, Mom looks happier, like maybe Gran won't think we stayed away too long after all. The baby starts doing some pre-crying in her baby seat. Dad and I invented the word *pre-crying*, which means the crying that comes right before the really loud crying. Mom isn't fussing with her because she wants me to know that this trip is about me having special time with Gran Nicholas, and not just for Gran to finally see the baby in real life. I heard Mom talking to Dad about it the day we left home. Mom said, "I want Olivia to know that this trip is about her having special time with Gran. Not just about the baby."

And Dad said, "I know, hon. You told me yesterday. And this morning."

Dad didn't come to Australia with us. He's at home, building a new room for the baby. He says it'll be ready when we get back.

Then I sort of remember another thing. It's something about the second floor, but I'm not sure exactly *what* about the second floor it is. I'm still squeezing that black pawn. It feels good in my hand.

"Is there something about the second floor?" I ask.

"Yes!" Gran says. "The second floor is where your room is. And your four-poster bed!"

But what I remember about the second floor is not a big bed with a canopy. I still don't know what it is, but it is not that.

It's . . .

It's . . .

"May I be excused?" I ask, already turning toward the stairs.

"I'll come up with you," Mom says. "Your

room used to be my room when I was a little girl, remember?"

I stop, one hand on the railing of the carpeted stairs that I used to bump down. For some reason, I think I'm supposed to go up alone. I glance at Beth Ann, who is still wiggling in her seat. Our eyes meet. As if she knows what I'm thinking, she quits her pre-crying and makes her *someone feed me* whimper. Mom turns toward her, torn between the two of us. I zoom up the stairs.

The doors along the upstairs hallway are open. I peek into what must be Gran's room, where a patchwork quilt is pulled over the bed. I pass the bathroom, where soaps in the shapes of ducks and chicks pretend to march along the counter toward the sink. By the time I reach the last room—*my* room—I'm almost running. I'm not sure why.

Then I see the closet. I still don't remember the bed, or the bright pink curtains. But I remember this closet. It's small—the door seems like only half a door, and there can't be much room on the other side.

I think I left something inside. Something really, really important.

My hand reaches for the doorknob. I know exactly where the light cord is, and I watch my hand reach out and pull it. The light flickers on.

Here is what I see:

1. A high shelf, jammed with shoeboxes and falling-down stacks of old comic books.

2. Below that, clothes on hangers dangle from a bar. There's a tutu with sequins and a few summer dresses for someone a lot smaller than me. Maybe Gran is keeping them for Beth Ann in a long, long time. Right now, Beth Ann is so small she can barely keep a shirt on.

One shoulder is always falling out of the neck hole. If I try to fix it, she cries.

3. On the floor, under the little dresses, a Lego pirate ship sits on the brown carpet. It has four sails and a mast and a lookout tower and even a swimming pool. It must have taken a long time to build.

4. Next to the pirate ship is a thick, old dictionary.

5. And standing on top of the dictionary is a small zombie wearing a chicken suit. He's rubbing his eyes, a Lego pirate clutched in one green hand. When his eyes adjust to the light, he uses them to look me up and down.

Then he says, "You're back. Took you long enough."

CHAPTER TWO

BOB

Her brown hair is longer and her cheeks are less round, but I know it's her. Livy. She told me to wait here, and I waited. Five years is a long time to hang out in a closet, but what else did I have going on? Not much, I'll tell you that.

Here are some of the things I did while I awaited her return:

1. Counted to 987,654,321. Six times.

2. Built a Lego pirate ship. Sixty-three times. In the dark.

3. Played chess against a Lego pirate monkey and still lost most of the time.

4. Tried to do the hokey pokey like Livy had taught me, but there's not much room to turn oneself around in this narrow closet without hitting the walls.

5. Cried. But only once.

6. Okay, twice. Each day. But only for the first year.

7. Meditated a few times after hearing Gran play a self-help tape on the benefits of calming the mind. This was actually not bad even though my legs cramped from sitting cross-legged.

8. Took a lot of naps, some lasting a few weeks at a time.

9. Thought of all the reasons that might explain why Livy didn't come back for me.

a) She was abducted by aliens. (But I am not convinced aliens exist. Zombies, yes; other monsters, probably; but aliens . . . not sure.)

b) Her family won the Saturday Lotto and went on the world's longest world tour. (If so, she could have stopped here to pick me up. I am small enough to fit in an overhead bin, and I do enjoy a nice salty peanut snack.)

c) She discovered an ancient mummy in Egypt and got busy giving interviews. (But I think I would have heard Gran Nicholas talk about this on the phone. Gran is a loud talker, and I have excellent hearing.)

d) She got scared. (But Livy is the bravest person I've ever met.)

e) She just didn't like me anymore. (This is the one that led to the crying.)

But now she stands before me and she looks so sorry and surprised that it is hard to be mad at her. I still am, but less. "You are all grown up," I say, letting the hand holding the Lego pirate swing behind my back.

She flips her hair over one shoulder. "Almost eleven."

"You are a lot taller and your face is not as mushy."

She reaches out a hand toward me but then lets it fall back. "I'm so sorry."

"You told me to wait for you in the closet. You said you'd be right back."

She tilts her head at me, just like she used to do before when she was trying to puzzle something out. "Did I really say I'd be right back?"

I consider this. "Well, you did say you'd see me soon. Five years isn't soon. It isn't even soon-*ish*."

Livy looks at her feet. "I can't remember anything. Honestly."

I do not reply. What can I say? All I did for five years was remember, and all she did was forget.

I narrow my eyes at her. This is not easy, because I don't actually have eyelids. I focus on looking skeptical and nonplussed. I know words like *skeptical* and *nonplussed* and a whole lot more because for twenty-six minutes each afternoon a shaft of sunlight shines through the doorframe of the closet and I read the dictionary. If I'd known about the light, I'd have gotten further than the *T*s.

She takes in my firm stance and my disapproving expression and my toes, tapping on the carpet. I am laying on the guilt trip pretty heavy. Then she rolls her eyes and puts her hands on her hips.

"I was *five*."

We hold each other's gazes until I sigh. She's right, of course. How can I blame her? She was this tiny slip of a girl, barely old enough to write her own name and tie her own shoes. I was ten at the time. For the record, I am still ten. I've always been ten, as far as I know.

Still, Livy was the kind of five-year-old who could get things done.

Wasn't it Livy who found me and saved me?

Wasn't it Livy who made me the chicken suit?

And taught me to walk in it?

Wasn't it Livy who promised she'd help me find my way home?

Five years is a long time to wait. But if she could do all that when she was little, she must be able to do much more now. Maybe this time, she will find my answers. Maybe this time, she will get me home.

CHAPTER THREE

LIVY

The zombie must have decided to forgive me because he (it?) is smiling at me now. But it is a smile like when you have decided to smile, not the kind of smile that just happens on its own.

This is what a smiling zombie looks like:

1. Short.

2. Green skin. Not grass green, more like inside-an-avocado green.

3. No hair, unless you count one long

eyebrow and the patchy fuzz growing on the top of his head.

4. Pretty skinny. I can see one knobby knee sticking out of the chicken suit where a seam has come undone.

5. Big melted-chocolate brown eyes.

6. No eyelids.

7. Smooth skin, at least the parts I can see.

8. A nose.

9. White teeth.

10. Lips turned up at the ends. Like I said, it was a potentially fake smile.

"Is that a . . . chicken suit?" I ask. It doesn't actually make him look anything like a chicken. In fact, don't ask me how I even know it's a chicken suit.

He sniffs. "Of course. It's THE chicken suit. The one you made for me." He reaches behind his neck and yanks the hood up. It's just some orangey cloth with glued-on feathers and an oversized red-felt chicken comb stuck on top of the hood. It looks like a little kid cut it out with bad scissors and glued it there.

I point at him. "I made . . . that?"

He tilts his head, and the red-felt chicken comb flops to one side. "Of course you made it! I didn't even know what a chicken WAS before I met you."

I learned about chicken combs in kindergarten when our class visited a farm. There was a huge rooster there named Queen. How come I remember the name of a rooster I met in kindergarten, but I don't remember . . . this?

"Why are you wearing a chicken suit? In here." In the closet, I meant, where he seems to live.

He sniffs again. "I am wearing it so that I will be ready." He hikes up one side of the thing, and the other side droops toward the floor.

"Ready for what?"

He gives me a long stare, and I figure this is another thing I'm supposed to remember.

"And why's it like—half on, half off? It reminds me of this kid in my class last year who always wore his coat with one arm pulled out of the sleeve."

"If you must know, I started to remove it about a year ago. I thought I might as well change clothes. But I'm afraid my left foot might be detached. There was an unfortunate incident involving the dictionary."

"You were attacked by a dictionary?"

"I didn't say that. It was more of a *tipping-over*." He glares at the dictionary, then strokes it like it's a pet rabbit or something. "Zombie parts detach very easily, you know. If I take the rest of the chicken suit off, the foot may peel right off with it!"

I eye him carefully. "What's your name?" I ask.

The zombie drops something on the floor. I

look down at his feet and see the Lego pirate. The pirate's hat has fallen off, and his little arms are stretched out toward it like he's trying to get it back. When I look up, the zombie has that mad look on his face again.

"You don't remember my *name*?" he asks. Then I realize he isn't mad. His feelings are hurt.

This is how a zombie looks when his feelings are hurt:

1. Pretty much the same as before, except the one eyebrow goes up and both sides of the mouth go down.

"I'm sure I'll remember it," I say quickly, "but if you tell me now, I'll know it sooner."

"I don't think I will," the zombie says. "I think I'll let you remember it, since you're so great at remembering things."

"Olivia!" It's Mom, calling from downstairs. "Lunchtime!"

"That's me," I tell the zombie. "I'm Olivia. People call me Livy."

He rolls his eyes. "I know *your* name!" Then he uses one foot to nudge the Lego pirate toward his ship. He does the same with the pirate's black hat. "The small pieces are really easy to lose," he mumbles.

"Olivia!" Mom calls again. Her voice is closer this time.

"I have to go eat," I say. "But I'll be back." I pull the light cord and close the closet door.

"I've heard *that* before," he mutters from the other side.

Gran has made ham-and-cheese sandwiches with pickles. Mom must have told her that it's my second-favorite lunch, after tacos. She pours us glasses of milk.

"To rain," Gran says, raising her glass.

Mom glances at me and then raises her glass. "To rain!" she says.

Then they look at me, so I say it, too.

Beth Ann can't even hold a glass. She just points at Gran's nose. She likes to point at people's noses.

It hasn't rained in Gran's town for a long, long time, which is bad. It's called a drought. It's bad for the plants, bad for the animals, and bad for the people who live around here. Mom says the drought is why Gran doesn't have horses anymore. She couldn't feed them because her grass stopped growing. She has to share water with her neighbors, and she only gets a little bit. Mom says she'll show me how to brush my teeth a special way so that I don't waste any.

"Livy," Gran says. "When your mom leaves and it's just the two of us, I thought maybe you and I could make a cake." She shows me a fat cookbook called *Women's Weekly Children's Birthday Cookbook*.

"Livy, this is the best cake cookbook on the planet!" Mom says.

Cake sounds good. But I have a zombie waiting for me upstairs. And I don't really want to think about Mom leaving.

And so I say it sounds great.

Lunch is pretty quick because Beth Ann gets right down to what Dad calls her "job," which is crying. Yes, crying is her job. And she's really good at it. No one even bothers trying to talk when she cries because she's so loud. Gran rubs Beth Ann's back while we put our heads down and eat. When I've finished my sandwich, my pickle, and Mom's pickle, I shout over the crying to say I'm going upstairs to read in the canopy bed, and Mom shouts back "Great idea!" and says she'll help me find a book.

I talk really loudly in the upstairs hall so that the zombie will know I'm not alone. When we walk into my room, the closet door is closed and there is no sign of him.

Mom puts her hand on my shoulder and

leads me to a bookshelf against the far wall. "These were all mine," she says. I tilt my head to read a few titles: *Alice in Wonderland*, which of course I've heard of, and *Snugglepot and Cuddlepie*, which I haven't. Mom picks out a book with a strange cover: one half of a smiling girl, and one half of a knight wearing black armor, lined up so that they look like the two sides of one person.

"*Half Magic!*" she says. "I loved this when I was your age. Just think, Olivia, when you were here before, you couldn't even read. Time goes so quickly."

I lie on the bed and pretend to love Mom's book right away, even though it usually takes me a little while to love a book. She gives me a quick hug and goes back downstairs, where Beth Ann is still crying.

I run to the closet. The zombie is hovering over the pirate ship again, this time with a Lego monkey in his hand. He drops the monkey and puts his hands over his ears.

"What," he asks, "is that horrible noise? Close the door!"

I tell him it is only the baby, doing her middle-of-the-night crying.

"Is it the middle of the night?" he asks. "It doesn't feel like the middle of the night, though I admit that a closet is not the best place to decide what time it is. There is a certain time-lessness to closets. This one, anyway."

"It's the middle of the night in Massachu-setts," I tell him. "Gran's house is fourteen hours ahead of Massachusetts time."

"Well," he says, "I guess your baby must be very good at math. But I wish you would make her stop."

"It's annoying, but it's her job," I tell him. "And she's not *my* baby."

Although I did name her. Mom and Dad let me because they read a book that said it might help with my "adjustment" to being a big sister. I have no idea why I named her Beth Ann. They probably should have named her themselves.

Downstairs, the phone starts ringing. Gran Nicholas has a really loud phone because her hearing isn't so great. You can hear her phone ringing even when Beth Ann is crying.

When I talk to Gran Nicholas on the phone at home, Mom always stands right behind me and tells me to speak up. And Gran always says, "Tell your mother I can hear you just fine. I've got my ears on." That's what she calls her hearing aids, her "ears."

I guess the phone was for Mom, because now she's yelling into it and laughing.

"My mom hasn't seen her friends in five years," I tell the zombie.

He looks up. "Me neither."

"Do you have friends?" I ask him. "Friends—like you?"

"That," he says, "is what we were trying to find out. Remember?"

I'm tired of saying everything I don't remember. Instead, I point to his foot, the one inside the chicken suit. "Can you wiggle it?"

"I think so." I see the bottom of the chicken suit move, and one feather flutters off. He sneezes.

"Take the suit off," I say. "I bet your foot's totally fine."

"No!" he says quickly. "I'm—not in the mood."

"You're scared."

"I'm not scared. I just don't feel like it."

"What kind of zombie gets scared about taking off a chicken suit? I thought zombies were strong and powerful."

"Are they?" He looks up at me.

"You really never met another zombie?"

He shakes his head.

"But what about your parents?"

He is quiet now, concentrating on attaching the little plastic monkey to the pirate ship's mainsail. "Two hands," he tells the monkey. "We don't want you to fall off and get lost like poor Mr. Parrot."

This zombie has definitely spent too much time alone. "You don't have parents?" I ask.

He rolls his eyes. "We've been *over* this," he says. "No parents that I know of. No idea who I am. No idea why I was mixed up with your gran's chickens. No idea where I came from. Or how to get back."

"Then how do you know you're a zombie in the first place?"

"The same way I know a lot of things. YOU told me."

"Me? You mean—before? When I was five? I didn't know anything!" I blink a few times and take a long look at him. Why did I even *think* he was a zombie when I opened the closet door this morning? He's green and his clothes are kind of ratty, but does that make him a zombie? I'm pretty sure five-year-old me confused both of us.

"Listen," I say. "What if you're not a zombie?"

"I AM a zombie. I know I am. That's why I don't need to eat or sleep much. And that's why I'm so careful about my parts falling off!"

"But *have* any parts fallen off? Ever?"

He glances at the foot inside the chicken suit. "I'm not sure."

"Hold out your hand."

He holds out one hand.

"Look," I say. "Five fingers."

He wiggles them. "But how do you know how many I started with? Maybe I had six. Maybe I had eight!"

I shake my head. "Take that foot out of the chicken suit. I bet you a hundred dollars it's still attached."

He hugs the ratty-looking orange cloth to his body. "No."

This kind of reminds me of the time Suzanna Hopewell kicked me in the face with her soccer cleats. Not on purpose—we were both going after the ball, I tripped and rolled, and the bottom of her shoe scraped the whole side of my face. I covered my cheek with both hands and wouldn't let anyone look. I was too afraid of what they might see. Finally, Dad blocked the door to the field house bathroom so that I could look in the mirror, by myself. There was a big gash next to my ear, but it wasn't as bad as what I had been imagining. I got fourteen stitches, and Mom bought me a bag of candy corn almost as big as my backpack.

"Do you want to look at it by yourself?" I ask him.

He grunts and says, "If I wanted to look at it *by myself*, don't you think I would have done it by now?"

I have an idea. I point at the huge dictionary. "Let's look up *zombie* and see if you match the definition."

He looks worried. "But what if I'm not a zombie? What happens then?"

"If you're not a zombie, then your foot is

still connected to your body. That would be good news, right?"

He thinks and then nods. He puts two hands on the dictionary and pushes it along the floor, out of the closet, to where I'm standing.

I sit on the rug, open the dictionary to *A*, and then wish I'd started at the back. I have to move the pages in big clumps with both hands. The "probably-not-really-a-zombie" waits patiently.

I get to *Z* and trail my finger down the pages like I've seen Dad do. I move past *zest* (spirited enjoyment, gusto), past *zodiac* (a celestial path), and land on *zombie*. We lean in together to read the definition.

CHAPTER FOUR

BOB

zombie [zom-bee]: noun.
A dead body brought back to life.

A dead body!" We both jump away from
the book. Livy trips on the rug, and we
fall into a heap.

"I'm not *dead!*" I insist, my face pushed
straight into the rug. I unscramble my legs and
pick up the dictionary. It is not heavy for me. I
flip to the *D* pages, which I already went through
during my first year in the closet, after I taught
myself how to read.

I read aloud, "*Dead [ded]: adjective. Lacking power*

to move, feel, or respond. Incapable of being stirred emotionally."

"You are definitely moving," she observes. "Even your foot."

I stand up, shimmy, and turn in a circle to prove her right.

She reaches out and pinches that sensitive spot under my elbow. "Ouch!"

"You feel and respond," she says.

I rub my arm. "I am very sensitive," I say, raising my chin. "I've always been like that."

"Always?" she asks. "Because I thought you didn't know anything about yourself."

I shake my head. "I know I feel sad when Gran worries into the phone about missing the rain. I know I like salty snacks and avocados on toast and warm tea because you gave me that for breakfast last time, only you called it *brekkie*, which is what Gran calls it, and we both agreed we liked the sound of it. I also like pirates and the color orange and I know my name. But that does not tell me where I came from or what I am."

"Can you *please* tell me your name?" she begs. "Is it . . . Bertram?"

I shake my head. "Do I look like a Bertram?"

"Not really," she admits. "Throckmorton? Lachlan?"

I shake my head. "*Lachlan?*"

She shrugs. "I remember that's a common name for boys here in Australia."

"*That* you remember?"

"Can't you just tell me?"

"First you have to promise not to laugh."

She makes an *X* over her heart.

So I tell her. "It's Bob."

Her lips quiver at the corners, but she keeps her word and does not laugh.

"I know it's not a very exciting name for a zombie, but it's all I've got."

"You're not a zombie, though. You could be almost anything."

I brighten. She's right! I think about the possibilities. I know I'm not human—maybe I'm *super*human! "Livy! I could be the Hulk or Green Lantern!"

I don't just read the dictionary. Sometimes I read the superhero comic books on the top shelf that I have to stand on the dictionary to reach. I never thought I might *be* one of them before!

Livy looks me up and down. "The color's right. But the Hulk needs to be angry before he turns green. Are you angry?"

Well, I'm still more than a little ticked off about everything, but not angry. I shake my head.

"Doesn't the Green Lantern always wear a special ring?"

I look down at my bare hands and sigh. "I guess I'm not the Green Lantern."

"Don't feel too bad," Livy says. "Whatever you are you're still pretty cool."

I haven't gotten a compliment in a long time. Five years, to be exact. It feels nice. I want to tell her there are plenty of other super-heroes I could be even though they're not green, but she is tapping the cover of the dictionary now.

"I wonder if there's a book where we can look up what you *are*, instead of what you're not."

We both glance over at the bookshelf.

Livy moves her hand along the edges of the books like she's looking for one in particular, but then shakes her head. "If there is, we don't have it. But we'll figure this out."

A look crosses her face, a familiar look. She is concentrating. I like that look.

"All right," she says, facing me. "First things first. I need you to tell me everything that hap-pened when I was here last time."

I open my mouth, but she holds up her hand.

"Not right now. My mother's going to come

up any minute to check on me. Can you hide again? If she sees you, she'll totally freak out."

"Maybe I'm like the Invisible Girl from the Fantastic Four," I say, stalling. I really don't want to get back in that closet. "Maybe I can turn invisible even though I'm not a girl."

"Can you?" she asks, tapping her foot.

I squeeze my eyes shut and practice being not seen. I open one eye. "Well? Can you see me?"

"Yes, Bob, I can see you."

She said my name. *Bob*. It makes me feel . . . well, *seen*. And heard. Like I'm a person. Or whatever I am. I'm glad I'm not invisible after all.

I hear her mother approaching the door. Uh-oh! With my super-hearing I should have known she was coming. I was too busy basking in the glow of hearing my name. The Great and Powerful Bob. The Bobster. His Bobness.

Luckily her mom stops for a second outside

the door to knock. She is a very polite mom. Not that I know many moms. Or *any* moms.

I take the opportunity to fling myself back into the closet. What choice do I have? Livy sticks out her foot and pushes the closet door closed just as the bedroom door opens. My heart is beating really fast.

Hey! That's more proof that I'm not dead! Dead things don't have heartbeats.

"Are you up for a walk, Olivia?" her mother asks. "Let's go get some fresh air."

Livy hesitates, but then, extra loud, says, "Okay, let's go for a walk." She doesn't have to talk loud for my benefit. I have excellent hearing when I pay attention. I've learned most of what I know about the outside world from listening to Gran Nicholas's television through the closet wall.

Like now I hear their feet moving across the carpet toward the door. Then one set stops. "What's this?" her mother asks.

"That?" Livy says. "Oh, just some feathers I found in the closet. An old art project I must have started last time I was here."

I suddenly realize my elbow feels bare and breezy. I reach around, and sure enough, some feathers are missing from my chicken outfit! I feel wrong without them. Like I'm not me. I hold my breath. I hope her mother doesn't take them!

"I'm glad you're remembering some things from last time," she tells Livy. "It's always nice to return somewhere you've already made happy memories."

Silence. Is she doing something with the feathers? What is she doing? I am itching to peek out, but there is no keyhole in the door, because who would lock a closet?

"You can just leave those feathers on the bed," Livy finally says.

"Of course," her mother says. "We can see the animals and I'll show you the well I built

with my dad when I was your age. You weren't allowed to go near it last time because you were too small." Her voice fades as they go down the stairs.

The last thing I hear is Livy saying, "I don't remember having to stay away from a well."

But *I* do. I remember her making a wide circle around that well every time we went out to the backyard. She kept me far away from it, too. She was good at looking out for me.

When I hear the kitchen's back door slam shut downstairs, I fling open the closet door and grab my feathers off the bed. I am glad that my foot is not detached after all, because that would make it hard to run.

I hold the feathers to my arm. I will have to ask Livy to bring me glue or sticky tape when she returns. Feeling like myself again, I snuggle down into my sleep corner for a nap. Every few months I like to sleep for an hour or two. It relaxes me when I'm stressed.

When I wake up I can tell through the sliver of space in the doorframe that it is dark. I sit upright. That was a long nap! Livy didn't return in all this time? Has she left me AGAIN?

I throw open the door. Under the bedsheet is the unmistakable outline of my old friend. Unless . . . unless she stuffed pillows in there to make it *look* like her. She told me she did that once at home and then snuck downstairs for an ice pop.

I'd like to try an ice pop someday.

I poke one small green finger at the lump in her bed.

Snore.

Phew. Pillows don't snore, so that's a good sign. I turn back to the closet and nearly trip over the tray of baked beans, a bag of potato chips, and an orange fizzy drink that is sitting right there. Three new foods to try! Hurrah!

The note taped to the side of the bag of chips says:

Dear Bob (also known as the not-zombie),

I didn't want to wake you. Plus I'm all jet-lagged and needed to sleep. Strange word (jet-lagged, not sleep, which isn't that strange a word at all). Anyway, I'm sorry again for the wait and for the forgetting. We will figure out what you are, I promise.

Your friend, Olivia (also known as Livy)

I beam. I knew Old Livy was still in there somewhere, even though new Livy might have forgotten her.

I carefully peel the note off the chips and use the tape to stick the feathers back on. Then I settle down to my feast, wishing Livy was awake to share it with me. Humans are strange. Sleeping half their lives away like that. Not that my life has been so exciting these past five years.

The beans are excellent.

CHAPTER FIVE

LIVY

It's hard to sleep through the night in Australia, especially when Bob is eating potato chips right next to the bed. I wouldn't say this to his face, but Bob looks sort of creature-ish, as if he might scarf down his food like a dog or something, but from the sound of it, he's actually a very neat eater. The problem is that he crinkles the bag a lot.

I'm under the covers, thinking. I like to think like this sometimes when nobody knows I'm awake. And what I'm thinking about is what to do about Bob.

Bob thinks I can help him find his home. He waited for me in Gran's closet for *five years*. But where did he come from?

The first thing Bob can remember is the chicken coop. So maybe we should start there. We've got to figure out how Bob can go outside without anyone seeing him. How does a green guy blend in to a place where nothing is green anymore? Everything around Gran's house is kind of dry and brownish.

I don't think the chicken suit is going to work. How could Bob ever pass for a chicken?

The bag-crinkling stops suddenly. Did I say that out loud? I sit up.

Bob is standing right next to the bed, looking at me with sad eyes. He's just tall enough to rest his green chin on the mattress.

"Don't worry," Bob says. "This chicken suit has never failed me."

I look at him. He's got the hood on and zipped everything up, but one shoulder of

the chicken suit has slipped off again. He's squeezing the potato chip bag. I see that he taped a couple of loose feathers to his arm, and they're sticking out in three directions, in a way that a real chicken's feathers would never, ever do.

But I decide to be optimistic. Dad says being optimistic is when you decide everything will probably be okay, even if you don't exactly know how. Like when my soccer team was losing 7–0, and Dad had us put our hands together and chant, "We are champions!" before the second half started.

So I smile.

Bob smiles back. "That's better. You look almost like the old Livy!" And he pops the top of his orange soda.

"There's only one me, Bob."

He slurps.

Then he burps.

I sigh. We lost that soccer game. I think the final score was 12–1.

Only one more night until Mom leaves with Beth Ann. A bad feeling starts in my stomach. I tell it to go away, but that just makes it bigger.

I look at Bob again.

He's spent more than a thousand nights in this house without his mother. He's watching me, munching away. I want to promise that I'm going to get him home, wherever home is for Bob. But what if I can't?

Suddenly I'm looking at the back of him. Bob can move fast. The closet door closes behind him at the same moment the bedroom door swings open and Mom sticks her head in.

She smiles. "Didn't think you'd be able to sleep through those magpies. Aren't they amazing? They sound like that cute robot from the first Star Wars movie."

I listen, and there it is—a funny bird-warble from outside. A lot of bird-warbles, actually. They kind of *do* sound like R2-D2.

Mom sits on the edge of the bed and puts

one hand on my forehead like she's feeling for a fever. I want her to leave that hand there forever.

"You doing okay?" she asks.

"Sure," I tell her. We're probably both playing the same movies in our heads:

1. Me getting picked up from Maya's house at nine o'clock the last two times I tried to sleep over.

2. Me getting picked up in the middle of Audrey Miller's slumber party.

3. Me getting picked up from the school trip to Newport. That one was a long drive for Dad.

Ever since Beth Ann was born, I can't sleep without knowing Mom or Dad is there.

"I'll only be gone for six nights," Mom says. "And Gran is family."

"I know that."

"You should be fine," Mom says.

That only makes me feel worse. I flip over so that my face is in the pillow, even though it means that Mom takes her hand away. Because I know I should be fine. I know there's no reason to feel worried. But the stomachache shows up anyway.

Mom squeezes my shoulders and says, "My brave girl," which is the last thing I feel like. I feel her weight leave the bed. "Breakfast in a few minutes, sweetie."

As soon as she's gone, I hear the closet door open. I lift my head, and Bob is back where he was before. No food this time. Just big eyes.

"Bob," I say. "I'm not going to leave you alone again. I promise."

A few hours later, we're standing at the kitchen door, looking across Gran's yard to the chicken house. Mom has taken the baby into town for some shopping, and Gran has walked over to the neighbor's farm. In Massachusetts, it takes about thirty seconds to walk from our front door to the neighbor's house, but at Gran's it's a long walk.

It's a good thing no one's home, because Bob insisted on going down Gran's back stairs on his butt six times: It turns out we did have a name for it. It's called butt-bumping. And it hurts. Maybe I had more padding when I was five.

"Looks like the coast is clear," I say, scanning the dusty yard.

"I told you, it doesn't matter about the coast. The chicken suit works perfectly."

I can't even look at him. We've spent the last twenty minutes taping every loose feather in the closet to Bob's back, and the chicken suit looks dumber than ever.

"Don't think that way, Livy," Bob says. "We have to think positive thoughts."

I blink. "Are you reading my mind or something?" Because this is the second time that's happened.

He reaches up to poke my nose. "I am read-ing your *face*."

Deep breath. "Okay," I tell him. "Let's go."

We head out, just me and a small green mys-tery wearing a chicken suit, into the sunlight. Three steps across the yard, I glance down at Bob and burst out laughing.

"Now what?" he asks. "Why are you laughing?"

"I'm laughing at the way you're walking. Like this." I do some fast little jumps, pumping my knees up into the air and landing on my toes.

"But that is the quicksteps," Bob says, look-ing hurt.

"And what's this?" I demonstrate again, still doing the crazy knees while also kind of lunging to the left and then to the right.

He sniffs. "That is the side-to-side."

We start walking, but after a few steps I have to stop again, I'm laughing so hard. "What's this part for?" I stick my head as far out on my neck as I can, then pull it back: out, back, out, back.

"That is the head-poke," he says impatiently. "Am I doing something wrong? This is the chicken walk you taught me."

"Are you kidding? I have no idea how to walk like a chicken! No offense, but it's dorky."

"You *did* teach me. You watched the chickens, to see what they did. And then you taught me how to walk like a chicken. The *old* Livy taught me."

I look over at the chickens pecking in their chicken yard. "Really? Weird. Let me see it again."

Bob walks out in front of me, knees pumping, stepping left and right and pecking at the ground.

I glance at the chickens again, and then back at Bob. "You know what? That's actually a pretty good chicken walk." Because, I realize, it is.

I can see him smile, even though he is still

in full-on chicken mode. Bob smiles with his whole head. It makes the sun feel warmer.

"Yes," he says to the dirt. "It is a very good chicken walk that the old Livy taught me."

"There's only one me," I tell him.

"If you say so," he says.

"HALLOOO there!" There is a man walking toward us, down Gran's long driveway. It takes me a few seconds to notice the boy walking next to him. He's maybe six or seven.

I look at Bob and realize how crazy it was that we ever thought this could work. Because Bob is a green mystery creature covered in orange cloth, tape, and feathers, pecking—kind of desperately, now—in the dirt. I hope he'll just keep his face down—maybe I can pass him off as my strange little brother.

The man and the boy smile all the way to where we're standing.

"Hi!" I say, jumping and waving, as if I can distract them from Bob by acting like a weirdo.

The boy waves shyly and looks at his feet. The man booms, "You must be the famous Olivia!" His voice is super friendly, but his face is nervous. "You got big! I almost didn't recognize you." He's twisting a white envelope in his hands.

"Yes! I'm Livy!" I'm still jumping. I don't want him to take his eyes off me. If he sees Bob he might call the police or something.

"Hoppy little thing, aren't you?"

"Yes!" I say. "I'm kind of hoppy!" I start hopping on my right foot only. It must be working, because neither of them is looking at Bob.

He laughs, then catches himself and looks at the envelope in his hands. He seems surprised to see that it's bent, and starts trying to flatten it out. "Is your gran at home?"

"No!" I say, switching to my left foot and hopping a little faster. "She went over to the neighbor's!" The harder I hop, the harder Bob pecks in the dirt.

The man laughs again. "Well, we *are* the neighbors."

"Oh! Ha!" I switch back to the right foot.

"Is everything all right?" he asks. "You don't need anything, do you? Like—the toilet, maybe?"

In Australia they say *toilet* for *bathroom*. I know this because I have spent a lot of time back home trying to teach my mom *not* to say toilet for bathroom.

"No need for the toilet! Ha-ha! I'm just getting some exercise! Hopping is great exercise! This is how we exercise in the United States!" I don't let my eyes look at Bob, still pecking furiously.

"Exercise, huh? Must be something new. Well, we'll probably meet your gran in the road, I'm thinking. But if we don't, can you tell her that Danny and I came by to see her?"

This is when I notice that "Danny" is staring at Bob.

"Sure!" I say, switching legs again. "I'll tell her!"

"And"—he looks at the envelope in his hand like it's telling him something he doesn't want to hear—"could you give her this for me?"

"Okay." Still hopping, I reach out for the envelope. But then he pulls it back. "Never mind. I'll give it to her later. Let's go, Danny. We have cows to milk."

They start back down the driveway, and I see the man pat the small head of Danny, who looks back over his shoulder and quietly says two words: "Nice chicken."

I stop hopping and stand there, breathing hard. I look at Bob, his orange hood pulled tight to his round face, the red-felt chicken comb flopping over to one side of his head, and old chicken feathers stuck up and down his arms with big Xs of Scotch tape.

He stands up straight and puts one hand on

his hip. "I told you the suit works. It works every time."

But *how*?

"Forget the chicken walk," I say. "Let's just get to the chicken house before someone else shows up." I grab Bob's hand, and we run. His hand in my hand feels familiar and comfortable. Like a girl and her not-zombie-fake-chicken should.

The chickens are walking around in the chicken yard, which is fenced in with wire. They're walking back and forth in a group and pecking in the dirt. There are a lot of loose feathers around. Bob is shoving them into his pockets.

"Your chicken suit has pockets?" I ask.

"Of course."

I look a little more closely. In the daylight, this chicken suit looks very familiar.

"Are those my old pajamas?"

Bob nods. "Of course."

I remember them now, fuzzy orange pajamas with a hood. I guess that explains how I made Bob's chicken suit when I was only five. All I needed was a bottle of glue and a lot of feathers. And some red felt, for the chicken comb.

"Let's go back to the first thing you remember," I tell Bob. "Exactly where did I find you?"

He points to the little wooden chicken house that sits against one side of the fence. "In there."

Bob slips through the doorway without a problem, but for me it's a squeeze. Inside the chicken house there's barely room to stand up. There's not much light and not much to see— just water pans and straw and chicken poop. And more feathers.

"Anything look familiar?" I ask Bob.

He looks around. "Oh yes," he says. "Very familiar. It is just the way I remember it."

"It's kind of smelly," I say.

Bob nods.

"And this is where we met? For the first time?"

He thinks. "This place is the first thing I remember. About anything. This place, and you."

It's almost like he hatched from one of the chicken eggs. I take a long look at Bob. No way he came from a chicken.

"Maybe there's a passageway or something?"

Bob's face lights up. "Yes, a secret passage! To home!"

"You feel around over there," I tell him. "I'll check this side."

We both drop to our knees and start patting the ground. As soon as we start moving the straw around, a lot of gross dust goes up my nose and into my eyes. After a while, I hear Bob say, "I used the door, though."

"What?"

"The door." He points to it. "I used the door to come in. Not a secret passageway."

"Why didn't you say so?" I wipe my face, but my hands are so dirty that it just makes things worse. "It's really gross in here, Bob. Why did you come here in the first place? Do you think you were running away from something?"

Bob thinks, tilting his head so that his chicken comb flops in the other direction. "No," he says. "I came here because it was warm."

"Were you cold?"

"No," he says slowly. "*You* were cold."

"*I* was cold?"

"You were shivering."

"Why was I shivering?"

"Because it was almost winter. And you were soaking wet."

CHAPTER SIX

BOB

If I think back really hard I can still see the five-year-old Livy curled up on the straw, her long hair and orange pajamas matted with leaves, and a tiny frog stuck inside the hood.

"A *frog*?" she says when I tell her.

I nod, remembering the bright greenness of the frog. "It hopped out and landed on your nose, and when I shook you, you woke up, and then you laughed when you saw it." I don't add that when she saw *me*, she stopped laughing.

"Why was I sleeping if I was soaking wet in a chicken coop? Was it raining?"

I shake my head. "It was sunny." I remember the early-morning light through the slats in the roof, and the dust hanging in the air. "And you took a long time to wake up."

"But I thought I was the one who saved *you*."

I shake my head again. "That came later."

She sighs. The old Livy never sighed. This one sighs a lot.

A car door shuts. Livy jumps up and peers through the window. "Mom's back! Stay in here until we're out of the way, and then you can run back to the house. Okay?"

She still doesn't trust the chicken suit.

She ducks through the door before I can say that I don't want her to go. Now I'm all alone with the real chickens, who look at me suspiciously. I cross my arms and sit in the corner, the same corner where she was all wet.

A minute later I can hear Livy laughing. I risk peeking out the window. Gran has joined her and her mom and the baby. They're feeding cucumbers and carrots to the pigs! Gran shows

Livy how to hold the vegetables so the pigs don't nibble her fingers. "Your dad will love this," her mom says, snapping pictures. "Our little farm girl!"

I slump back down. *I* want to be a little farm girl! Well, a farm *not-zombie*! I haven't been outside in FIVE YEARS. *I* should get to feed the pigs. And run in the grass. And stare up at the wide, blue sky that I'd almost forgotten existed. I should get to climb a tree if I feel like it. Why does Livy get to make all the decisions?

I don't like the way that one chicken over there keeps glancing at me. I think she is up to no good. She looks like the kind of chicken who could peck your eye out and not even feel bad about it.

I scurry out into the sun. Now everyone is laughing at how the pigs' tails are like little curly question marks and how they would go *boing* if you unwound them. I do my best chicken walk toward them but then stop before I get too close. Livy will be so upset if she sees me. Maybe this was a bad idea. I glance around, looking for cover, and spot the well. This time Livy can't keep me from checking it out. I change course and dart behind it. I am now officially a rule breaker.

The stones that surround the well are warm from the sun. Leaning against them feels nice on my back. My feet feel funny, though, like cold and hot at the same time. The funny, tingly feeling starts there, but then it goes higher and higher till it reaches my head. Is this what Spider-Man's spider-sense feels like? Or was it the beans?

I bet it was the beans.

I turn to my left. I am not alone at the well.

Danny, the old man had called him earlier. He is sitting against the low wall with his knees pulled up to his chest and a book at his side. He sees me and his eyes widen in surprise, but it's not the kind of surprise like if you just saw a not-zombie, more like the kind where you just saw a big chicken.

He has pink icing around his lips and he's been crying. I want to ask if he's okay, but chickens do not talk. So instead I peck at the ground and think that life can't be all that bad if you just ate something with pink icing on it.

"You're lucky to be a chicken," the boy says, angrily wiping at his eyes with the back of his hand. "Your life is so easy."

Easy peasy lemon squeezy, I want to tell him. Old Livy used to say that. I've been waiting for a chance to use it, but now is not that time. Plus, my life is SO NOT EASY.

He sniffles, then reaches out and strokes my fake chicken comb. I hold my breath.

This suit works REALLY WELL.

"Some days I wish I could be a chicken," Danny says. "Things are hard when you're a person. Grandpop is going to lose his farm soon. Nothing grows anymore."

He keeps petting my head.

I can't talk to tell him that things will be okay (and how do I know they will?), so I just give him a gentle nudge on the chin and hope he understands.

A shadow falls over us, and I look up. Dark clouds have rolled in, hiding the sun. Danny lets his hand fall from my head and stops crying. "Clouds," he says, his voice full of wonder. Then he stands up and shouts. "Rain clouds!"

"Shhh!" I know chickens don't shush people, but I can't help it.

But it's too late—Livy and the whole family are staring right at us.

Livy's eyes dart wildly between me and Danny.

"Look at the clouds!" she shouts, stabbing her finger upward a bit too frantically. But it works. Everyone looks up, even the baby, which gives me a chance to escape. But I don't. Something holds me there.

We hear thunder, and everyone cheers. Gran lifts the baby up to the sky and hops around and *woo-hoos*! She's stronger than she looks! Livy's mom throws her arms around Livy and squeezes. At this moment, I could take off the chicken suit and do a naked somersault, and not one of them would notice.

From behind her mom's back, Livy waves for me to go to the house. Danny has run over to join the whooping and dancing, and I want more than anything to join in, too. But I do my best chicken walk toward the back door.

Giant blobs of water plonk onto my head, splash on my face, and roll down toward my mouth. Rain! It's a little weird. Not bad necessarily, just different. Not sure what all the fuss is about, frankly. By the time I've made it to the door, the rain has stopped and the clouds are rolling away.

That was fast.

The cheering stops as if someone has thrown a switch. Everyone is quiet. Livy is frowning and that makes me sad. I hear her mom say that the baby needs to get into some dry clothes. I'd better get upstairs before they come in.

Also, I'm pretty sure there are some potato chips left in the bottom of the bag.

CHAPTER SEVEN

LIVY

"Open the door already! You've been in there for fifteen minutes." It's taken me ten minutes of talking through the closet door to convince Bob to take off his soaking-wet chicken suit and change into something dry, and now he won't come out.

"No."

"Come on." I try to turn the knob, but he must be holding it on the other side.

"No."

"Come *on*!"

Bob doesn't answer at first. Then he says, "You do not say please very often, do you?" He sniffs. "Old Livy did not like to say please, either."

He's right. I don't like to say please. I don't mind the polite please, like when you want someone to pass you the mashed potatoes, but I don't like the begging kind of please.

"Please?" I say.

"I am considering it."

"Pretty please? How bad can it be?"

The door swings open, and there is Bob, arms crossed tightly over his narrow chest. He is wearing my old tutu. He looks smaller in the tutu than he did in the chicken suit.

"It's not so bad. At least both your feet are still attached," I say.

"It was this or a bathing suit," he says.

I probably would have gone with the bathing suit. That tutu looks itchy.

"Maybe you could get me something else to

wear? When you are in town tonight?" Bob's eyes shine. "In Gran's soap operas, someone is always going into town to shop."

"I'll try. But it might be hard to get my mom to buy me something in your size."

He looks at me. One side of the tutu sticks up in a funny way, like it's been pressed up against the closet wall for the last five years. That plus Bob's dead-serious look makes me want to hug him. But I don't.

Suddenly Bob smiles. "Do you have time for chess?"

"You play chess?"

He nods. "Your dad taught you, and you taught me."

A little wiggle at the back of my head tells me he's right.

"I'll set up the board!" Bob says, running to his closet. "I've been practicing by myself. I mean, technically, it has always been me against Mr. Monkey, but I make all his moves for him."

"Who usually wins?"

He scratches his head. "That's the other thing. We only have the white chess pieces, so we share them. And I always forget whose pieces are whose. I wish I could find the black ones."

"Black chess pieces?" I say. "I know where they are!"

"You do?" Bob does a little jump, which is really cute, because of the tutu. "Don't just stand there. Get them!"

When I get to the kitchen, Gran is standing by the window, reading a letter and frowning. "You've been up in your room a lot," she says, switching to a smile. "Everything all right? We're still making that cake tomorrow, right?"

"Yes! Everything is great. But do you know where those chess pieces are? The black ones you showed me yesterday?"

"Of course." She drops the letter on the kitchen table, next to a ripped-open white envelope, and I realize Gran is reading the letter that the neighbor was twisting in his hands this morning. He looked miserable when he was holding it, and now that Gran has it, she looks kind of miserable. Even though she's still smiling at me.

When Gran turns away, I tilt my head and read the words at the top of the page: BANK OF AUSTRALIA.

Gran holds the net bag of chess pieces out to me. "Do you remember trying to take these home last time you came? You had them all packed away in your backpack! Cutest thing."

"I did?"

She nods. "Your mom found them at the last minute, and they've been sitting in my kitchen drawer ever since. I'd challenge you to a game, but I can't find the white ones."

Upstairs, Bob is sitting cross-legged on the floor of my room, with the chessboard in front of him. All the white pieces are resting on their squares, the important pieces in the back row and the pawns lined up in front of them.

I start setting up my side of the board. Bob smiles at me and says, "Just like old times. You always have to be black."

"It's lucky," I tell him.

"But chess is not about luck," Bob says. "It's about recognizing the strength of the little guy."

"What are you talking about?"

He picks up a pawn and waves it at me. "Everyone underestimates the little guy. But the pawn is the key to the game."

I laugh. "Where are you getting this stuff?"

His face grows serious. "The pawn protects every other piece on the board," Bob says, "even though it can't make as many different moves. And if you can get it to the other side of the board safely, it becomes a much more powerful piece, like a knight or a queen." Then he smiles, slides his first pawn down the center of the board from e2 to e4, and says, "Let's see what you've learned in five years."

I move my own pawn out to c5 and watch his eyes get big when he realizes I'm doing the Sicilian Defense. I grin. "Game on, my not-zombie friend."

He beams. "You are a much better opponent than Mr. Monkey."

We've barely gotten started when I hear Mom calling up the stairs that it's time to go into town.

Bob looks up. "Don't forget I need something to wear."

"I'll try," I say.

"Don't forget about me," he says.

"I won't," I tell him.

"Promise?"

"Promise."

He picks up a black pawn from the board and hands it to me. "Put this in your pocket," he says.

"Why?"

"I don't know why. But it's important. It is what you always did before."

"Bob, I was *five* before. I probably did things for no reason at all."

"Please," Bob says, "just do it."

"Fine." I lean over and swipe a different black pawn from the board.

"No," Bob says. "It has to be this one. The one with the chip on the bottom."

He actually looks kind of worried, so I take the "special" pawn from him and stick it in my front jeans pocket. And then I give him a quick hug.

Bob is a good hugger. His arms go around my middle and he looks up at me with these eyes that remind me of Joanie, our neighbor's German shepherd back home. Sometimes when I'm sitting on my porch, Joanie comes over and puts her chin on my knee and looks at me just like Bob is doing now. Mom calls her "Lonely Joan." But I don't think Joan is lonely. I think she just has a way of knowing when a person needs cheering up.

I pat the pocket with the chess pawn in it. "I'll be back soon, Bob. As soon as I can. Then I'll finish beating you at chess."

I thought "town" would be a big place like ours at home, with coffee shops, stores, restaurants, and maybe a movie theater, but Gran's town turns out to be one street, with a stretch of stores on one side of the road and nothing but dirt and dead grass on the other. We start at one end and go slowly, stopping at each and every "shop," where Gran introduces us to whoever is behind the cash register.

Beth Ann did her four-o'clock crying in the car, so she's smiling now, and even willing to be passed over the counter and held by whoever is there.

"Do we have to go to every single place?" I whisper to Mom in the wool shop. Yarn is boring.

"Yes, we do," she says. "Gran is showing us around to her people."

Showing the baby around, more like.

I cheer up a little when the third store turns out to sell clothes. Because I wanted to go to a clothing store. I know I did, even though I can't remember exactly why.

"Can I get something?" I ask Mom.

"Maybe," she says. "Show me what you want."

But I can't remember what I want. I look around at all the stuff—it's nothing fancy, just different kinds of t-shirts and a few handmade things in baskets—and I can't even remember *why* I wanted to come here in the first place. It's like I'm reaching for something in my brain that isn't there anymore. And then Mom says the baby needs her diaper changed *right now*, and we're leaving the store before I can figure it out.

I wait with Gran while Mom changes the baby in the back of the car. Gran keeps looking across the road at the field of brown grass. It's cut very short. Back home, I love walking on cut grass with my bare feet, but this grass looks like it would hurt to walk on.

When Mom gets back with Beth Ann, we start moving faster because it turns out that a few of the stores have shut down. Gran stops in front of each one and tells Mom when it went out of business. The bookstore closed last summer. ("Ms. Penn, who used to run it, is living on next to nothing now. She always knew what book I needed to read.") The antiques shop closed just a few weeks ago. ("Who has money for knickknacks these days?")

I perk up when we walk into what Gran calls the "lolly shop." There's candy in big jugs all over the place. ("Thank goodness people can always find some change for something sweet!") The lady behind the counter hugs Mom, holds her arms out for the baby, and calls to me that I can pick any three things I want.

I walk slowly from bin to bin, taking a square

caramel in a clear wrapper because caramels are my favorite, then a sour cherry ball because they last a long time, and I'm still thinking about the third thing I should pick when the lady calls out—"Oh, I moved the licorice! It's in the corner now." And she points.

I hate licorice. Why is she telling me where the licorice is? I kind of smile at her and keep walking—chocolate? Gummy frog?

"Don't be shy," she calls. "I know it's your favorite."

Mom is smiling at me in a funny way, because she knows I hate licorice. We both know that the lady behind the counter must be mixing me up with someone else's grand-daughter who probably visited a long time ago, but now that Mom is looking I'll have to do the polite thing and take one. Which means no chocolate and no gummy frog.

"No charge for those!" the lady says happily when I have all three pieces in my hand: the caramel, the sour cherry ball, and the dreaded licorice. But Gran Nicholas insists on paying for the candy.

"Put those in your pocket for later," Mom tells me the second we step outside. "No candy until after dinner."

We finally get to the town's one restaurant, at the end of the street. It's really just a square room full of square tables, each one covered with a white paper tablecloth that hangs down on the sides. There's a little jar of loose crayons on each table. Mom gives a loud whoop and hugs the waitress hello for a long time, and then a girl about my age comes through a swinging door with a basket of bread, which she puts down on our table.

"I don't suppose you two remember each other," Gran says, smiling at the girl and then at me.

We both get shy.

The waitress says to me, "I've still got your drawing up, you know!"

My drawing?

Mom says, "Oh, how wonderful! Let's see!" She rubs my back as we all walk toward one of the walls, which I now see is covered with crayon drawings on paper tablecloths.

"I hang only the best," the waitress says. But now I'm wondering if maybe she's not the waitress. Maybe this is her restaurant? And maybe the girl standing next to me is her daughter? She points to a rectangle of paper that's pinned to the wall with four blue tacks. I glance at the other drawings on the wall—some of them are really good. This one, not so much.

It's baby stuff, a picture of a farm and two stick-figure girls with curly lines for hair and bright pink and purple triangle dresses. Yellow sun and green grass. The usual.

"Look at that delicious green grass," Gran says.

The waitress looks at Gran. "Dad told me that a letter came to our place by accident," she says. "It was from the bank?"

That twisted envelope. These are Gran's neighbors.

Gran says, "Never mind that letter. My family is here, and tonight is for celebrating. And nothing else. Livy, do you see who drew this gorgeous work of art?"

She points down near the bottom, where it says LIVY in big blue letters and SARAH in purple ones. I look at the girl again. She must be Sarah. She's not looking at the picture. She's looking at her feet.

"Remember the weekend you two spent together?" the waitress asks me. "Sarah spent the day with you at your gran's, and the next day you both came here to help me out. Sarah asked about you for the longest time after you left— 'When's Livy coming back? When's Livy coming back?'"

I glance at Sarah and see that her face is all red. "Well, hi again," I say.

"Hi," she whispers. Gran and Mom walk

over to our table and get the baby all set in her bundle-chair, which is her favorite place to sit, drool, and play with her fingers.

It feels better with Sarah as soon as the adults stop staring at us. "It's weird we drew this," I say. "I don't remember doing it."

"Me neither," she says. "Even though I see it every day. It's kind of cute."

I look at the drawing again. It is cute, actually—colorful, with horses and pigs in the yard, and a chicken house.

"You must have drawn the horses," I tell Sarah, "because I *still* can't draw a horse."

She laughs. "Maybe I did. I have no idea. And what the heck are those supposed to be?" She points to a clump of circles with stick feet.

"I think they're chickens," I say. "See the little red things on their heads?" And as I look more closely, I see that one chicken, unlike the others, has a carefully colored green face.

Weird.

I point to the drawing above ours, a black dog with a white chest, done in pencil. "*That* one is really good," I say.

She nods. "My little brother drew that. He's only seven, but he's definitely the official artist of the family."

"Danny?" That little kid drew this? "Wow."

"Yeah," she says.

"Hey, do you like licorice?" I ask Sarah. I reach into my pocket and take out my loot.

Sarah laughs. "You carry chess pieces around?"

I look at the pawn in my hand, and it's like a door swings open in my mind. *Bob. Bob* is that green chicken in our drawing. *Bob* is who I meant to buy clothes for! I promised him! And then I forgot him. Again.

I turn to Sarah. We were obviously friends when I was here last time. Maybe I told her something. It would be kind of great to have a partner. Because I can't leave Bob alone here again, and I don't actually have any idea how to get him home.

"Do you know . . . Bob?" I say.

"Who?"

"Um, Bob?" I wave one finger at the paper, in the general direction of the green-faced chicken.

"Was Bob a horse?" She frowns. "I hate to tell you this, but he might be gone now. Some people had to ship their horses off because of the drought."

"Oh."

"I'm really sorry," she says. And then our moms call us to the table to decide what we want for dinner.

"Can I run back to that store with the clothes?" I ask Mom. "I just remembered what I wanted. I'll be right back."

"What? No, we're eating now, Livy."

"Please? I . . . I'm cold."

"Sarah can lend you a jumper!" Sarah's

mom says. "She keeps an extra one in the back."

Jumper is Australian for sweatshirt, and it's hot in the restaurant, so I'm pretty miserable getting into Sarah's red hoodie, wondering how I could have forgotten Bob again. I stick the pawn in one pocket, along with the candy Sarah and I didn't have a chance to sneak.

Sarah takes the chair next to mine. She isn't shy anymore. In fact, she talks a lot. We're the only customers in the restaurant, except for one older couple at a table in the front window. I guess that means business isn't too good.

Our moms start telling stories about the crazy stuff boys in their class used to do, and Sarah and I keep laughing. It cools off as it gets later, so that I'm happy for the sweatshirt.

Our moms take about a hundred pictures of us.

After dinner, Sarah and her mom walk us back up the road to our car, and Mom asks if I still want to get something at the store. "A t-shirt, or something? It's not too late if you want to look."

I shrug and look into the store window as we pass by. Did I want a t-shirt? Why did I want a t-shirt?

Mom said the candy was for "after dinner," and this is after dinner. I reach into my pocket and come out with the caramel, the sour cherry ball, the licorice, and a chess piece—a black pawn.

The name comes back to me in a flash. *Bob.* And I realize that I've forgotten all about him. *Again.*

"Hey," Sarah says, "you never told me about the chess piece. Is it your lucky charm or something?"

I stare at that pawn and I finally get it: Something is wrong.

CHAPTER EIGHT

B🌀B

I learned a lot of things today on my adventure with Livy, but here's what I learned after she left: If you put a wet chicken suit in the clothes dryer, all the feathers will come off and the whole thing will shrink into a little ball.

The car pulls up outside just as I've rescued the last feather from the lint trap.

The tutu scratches at my legs as I climb the stairs with the whole mess in my arms. If I were Superman, I could have just used my heat lasers to dry it off, and it would be as good as new.

I wait in the closet. Waiting in a closet is not

so bad when you know someone will soon be opening it. Plus, being in here is kind of relaxing, like I don't have to worry about anything other than what's inside my head. I like filling my head. I flip the dictionary open to *U*. Now that I know where the light cord is, there'll be no stopping me.

I get up to *unicorn* before Livy swings open the door so wide the doorknob bangs into the opposite wall.

"That's gonna leave a mark," I say, shutting the book. "We can cross unicorn off the list of things I might be."

"I could have told you that," she says.

I hurry over to the bed to open the bag of clothes that is no doubt waiting for me there.

There is no bag. I purse my lips at her and wait for an explanation.

"So you'll never guess what happened to me in town," Livy says.

This better be good.

"I forgot about you!"

Only she sort of looks kind of excited about that, which is more than a little annoying.

"I forgot," she repeats. *"Again."*

I start to gnash my teeth, but my teeth are already small and kind of stubby. I put my hands on my hips instead. "Why are you happy about forgetting again?"

She shakes her head. "I'm not happy about the forgetting part, but now I think I understand *why* I forgot you the first time. I mean, I know I was really young, but let's face it, you're pretty memorable."

I have to agree there. I always thought I was pretty remarkable as far as mysterious creatures go.

She begins to pace the room. "When we left for dinner I was thinking about you. And the chicken house, and the clothes you wanted. But by the time we got into town I forgot all of it."

My eyes widen. I am less annoyed now, and more curious. "All of it?"

She nods.

I reach up and lay the back of my hand on Livy's forehead. "Maybe you have a fever?"

She shakes her head. "No, listen, it's not me. I think it's coming from you! You have a gift! I think you're . . . *magic*!"

I stare at her. "Oh great, so my magic is about people not being able to remember me? What kind of stinky magical gift is that?"

"It's not so bad," she insists. "It protects you from strangers, right?"

"I guess . . . but it makes *you* forget me, too."

"It would, yes! But I have something that reminds me." She dives into her pocket and pulls her hand out triumphantly to reveal . . . the chess piece?

I'm trying to keep up. "The chipped black pawn from the h7 square makes you remember me?"

"Yup! I must have figured this out when I was little. Gran said I tried to take it home last time. When I hold it, I remember you."

She lowers the pawn back onto the board so

it can continue its job of protecting the king. It wobbles as she sets it down. We both reach out to steady it, and our hands close on it at the same time. Our eyes meet in surprise. We'd clutched this same pawn between us before! Back then we'd laughed and rolled around the floor pretending to fight over it. But now we just stare at each other.

This action, this coming together, it linked us somehow. Livy is right about the magic. For some reason people forget about me when they get a certain distance away. But this pawn resists it.

This means Livy didn't really forget about me when she left five years ago! Well, she did, but not on purpose, because she didn't have the pawn. Knowing this makes a *huge* difference!

We finally let go. "See?" I tell her. "I was right about pawns being powerful!"

"Don't go getting a big head about it." She reaches into her pocket and pulls out a wrapped-up caramel and a piece of black licorice.

I grab for the licorice. "My favorite candy!"

"The lady at the store said I used to get it all the time."

I nod, chewing happily. "You did. You'd bring it back every time you went to town. You tried it once and said it tasted like dirt."

"That sounds like me," Livy says, popping the caramel into her mouth.

"Where did you find the black chess pieces, anyway?" I ask as I savor my delicious treat.

"They were downstairs with a bunch of other stuff Gran put out to show me." Her voice is a bit slurpy because of the caramel. "There was a green elephant, too, and a—"

"Rufus?" I jump up. "Gran found Rufus?"

"Huh? I'm not sure. I didn't ask his name."

"Green and soft? About the size of my head? Long trunk?" I start at my nose and swing my arm out like a trunk.

"Sounds like the one," she says.

I'm halfway out the door before she yanks me back.

"Hold on there, mister," she says.

"Oops, sorry. Will you get him for me?"

"Now?"

"Yes, please!"

I wait by the door, hopping up and down. Rufus! Rufus is back! I should probably act my age and not get excited about a stuffed animal. Then she walks in with him.

"Rufus!" I snatch him from her arms and hug him tight and sniff his head. "He smells just the same! Like cake and the outdoors!"

Livy half smiles and half rolls her eyes. "I'm glad you have your stuffed animal back."

I hold him out to her. "Oh no, he's not mine. Rufus is yours."

"Mine? I don't think so. I've never been an elephant person."

What a hurtful thing to say! I hug him again. "But when you were soaking wet in the chicken house, you had him in your arms."

She takes a step backward in surprise. "I did?"

"And he was wet, too."

"Rufus was wet?" Livy steps over to the window that looks out onto the yard. Her back is to me for a long time. When she turns around again her eyes are wide. "There's only one place in Gran's yard Rufus could have gotten wet. I think he fell in the well!"

CHAPTER NINE

LIVY

"Poor Rufus," Bob is saying, smoothing Rufus's short green elephant fur. "Did you fall in that deep, dark well? Bob will keep you safe now. You will never be in that dark well again."

I think Bob sometimes forgets that some of us are real live creatures and some of us are inanimate objects. It must have been because of all that time he spent in the closet with the Lego pirates, Mr. Monkey, and the parrot who got lost.

While Bob and Rufus are having their little reunion, I'm putting two and two together, as Dad says. Except it's more like trying to add the square root of seven and thirty-one to the fifth power.

Bob says I rescued him. But he also says he went to the chicken house in the *first* place because *I* was cold. Not him—*me*. And I was cold because I was wet. And now it turns out "poor Rufus" was also wet.

Gran Nicholas says I loved Rufus. I took him everywhere with me.

So I am beginning to wonder if maybe *I* am the one who fell in the well.

If maybe Bob saved *me*.

"Bob," I say.

He ignores me. He's sitting on the edge of my bed, talking to Rufus with his legs crossed and one side of his tutu sticking up. A strap is sliding down over one skinny green shoulder.

Wouldn't I remember falling into a well?

Maybe I hit my head. If I hit my head, I could have drowned. But—could Bob really have pulled me out? He doesn't look very strong.

"*Bob*," I say again.

He looks up. "Yes?"

"What if I didn't save you? What if you saved—*me*?"

"No," he says. "You saved *me*, Livy!"

"We have to go outside," I tell him. "Right now."

"Outside? It's almost bedtime. It's getting dark out." He looks at me with big eyes.

"I know," I say, throwing him Sarah's sweatshirt. I'm not too excited about the dark, either. "But this can't wait."

Five minutes later, we're at the far end of Gran's yard, where the stiff brown grass gives way to a lot of trees and rocky ground. It was easy to sneak out of the house, because Gran was on the phone and Mom was putting the baby to sleep.

We just walked out the front door (which Gran almost never uses) and then ran around to the back of the house and over to the well.

Bob runs up to it but doesn't touch it. He peers over the top (he has to stand on tiptoes) and then walks around the well slowly, looking as serious as a green guy can look in a tutu and a red sweatshirt so big on him that the zipper is swinging down by his ankles.

"What are we looking for?" he says. "Clues?"

"Bob, do you remember being here with me? With Rufus?"

He shakes his head and points to the chicken house. "I only remember the chickens."

But I do remember the well. Not just from yesterday's walk with Mom, when she talked (a lot) about collecting stones with her father to make the well wall. But from before, from when I was five. For instance, I know that if I walk around this well, I will see three little stones jutting out of the wall, one above the other.

Like three little steps that I might have tried to climb once.

I circle the well slowly, and there they are. I raise one knee and try to put my foot on the lowest little stone step. There's only room for my toes.

"Bob, you don't remember this place at all?"

He shakes his head again. And I'm out of memories. I definitely don't remember falling in. I force myself to look into the well's deep dark, and shudder.

"Let's go back to the chicken house," I say. It's the nearest thing to the well. That's where Bob thinks our story starts. Even though I'm feeling more and more sure that it starts exactly where we are now.

It takes less than a minute to walk to the chicken house. Bob stops just outside the fence and says he's not going in. "I don't like that chicken," he says, pointing at a big one. "She has it out for me."

"Bob, pay attention. This is where you watched me wake up, right?"

"Yes, Livy—inside, just like I told you."

"And then what?" I say.

"And then . . . you said you had to go to breakfast. That Gran would worry. I remember wondering what breakfast was. And you said it was usually something good, like pancakes or waffles. So I went with you." Bob is excited now, going up and down on his toes. It almost looks like a real ballerina move.

"Okay, show me how we got to the house."

"We walked, silly. I can't fly, as far as I know."

"Ha-ha. Show me exactly the way we went. Maybe we'll see something important."

He looks at the chickens and thinks for a second. "We walked along the edge of the grass, near the trees. You called it going 'the long way.'"

When Bob says *the long way*, I get this memory—like a picture flashing in my head—of

Gran's yard, all green, in the cold sunshine. And for the first time, I remember Rufus. I remember holding him, how soft he was and how I tucked him under one armpit to keep him safe while I used two hands to climb over a rock or a fallen-down tree trunk at the edge of the grass.

"Now we're getting somewhere. Show me the long way," I tell Bob.

We start picking our way along the edge of Gran's lawn, tripping over tree roots and stumbling on the little rocks that are loose in the dry dirt.

"Ouch!" Bob says, bending to rub his leg.

"It's not that bad," I say.

"Not for you, maybe. You're wearing pants."

I start laughing really hard. Because now Bob has a twig stuck to the back of his tutu. Against the dusky blue sky, it looks like he has a little tail.

Bob stops and turns to me. I can't see his face, only two glimmering eyes. "Stop!"

"Sorry!" I'm still laughing. When something hits my funny bone straight on, I just can't stop.

But Bob is suddenly serious. "Livy, it's our rock!" He points to a smooth gray-white rock. It's like a little table—almost a perfect rectangle, lying flat on the ground and reflecting the moonlight.

He hops up onto it. He's a good hopper, very springy. "Remember? You said it was a Sylvester rock! We had picnics here."

"You mean like the book? *Sylvester and the Magic Pebble*?" It actually does look a lot like the rock that Sylvester turned himself into. He wished to be a rock, to save himself from a lion. And then he couldn't wish himself back. His parents looked for him everywhere. That part always made me really sad.

"Livy, this is where you saved me that first day!"

"On this rock? Saved you from what?"

Bob drops his voice. "From a monster."

"Bob, really? A monster?"

"I was so scared I could barely move. My feet were stuck to the ground. You grabbed my hand and pulled me all the way to Gran's kitchen door. You saved me! Right here!"

"What kind of monster?"

"Oh! A toothsome and furry monster. Also, fast! A fast, toothsome, furry monster. And so loud! That screeching!" He covers his ears.

I pull his hands down. "Bob, you're safe. There's no monster here. Just tell me what happened."

"Maybe we should go inside now," Bob says.

"Bob. Maybe that monster was from *your world*. Maybe what you're remembering is a clue—it'll help us figure out where you came from!" I start hunting around the rock for more clues, but now it's almost too dark to see.

Bob is nodding, excited. "Yes! Maybe in *my* world, *I* am the people, like *you* are the people here. But in my world, there are monsters, and they run after us, screeching like this!"

And then Bob makes a noise.

I look up from my clue hunt. "*That's* the noise the monster made?"

"That's exactly what it sounded like! Do you remember it now? Have you ever heard such a horrible sound?"

Actually, I have. Because the sound Bob made was this: *meow.*

"Bob, I'm pretty sure that wasn't a monster. I think maybe it was a cat."

"A cat? Do you mean the small domesticated mammal? Catcher of rats and mice?"

"Um, I guess so? Most cats are cute and friendly. And they say meow."

"They do?" His look of terror disappears. "Well, it doesn't say anything about that in the dictionary! But still, it was very brave of you, Livy. To save me." He smiles. Then he pats the Sylvester rock. "And I always liked this rock!"

I think I get it. Bob saved me (from drowning) and then I saved him back (by walking away from a cat?). But none of this has helped us figure out anything about where Bob came from. I'm going to have to think of something else. I sit down hard on the Sylvester rock. It wobbles a little.

"Livy?"

"Yes?"

"Can we go home now? I want to introduce Rufus to Mr. Monkey."

We walk into the house the same way we left, and no one even knows we were gone. When we get upstairs, Bob lies down on the bed and insists that he needs Band-Aids for his scratched-up legs. I can't see any marks on him, but he says he heard a TV commercial once and he definitely needs one on each knee, so I go out to find some Band-Aids in the bathroom cabinet. When I come back into the room, I see Bob, still flat on the bed, with Mom standing over him. I freeze right where I am in the doorway.

"There you are," Mom says, turning to me.

Her eyes find the Band-Aid box in my hand. "What happened? Did you hurt yourself?"

I try not to look at Bob, who is lying very, very still and staring straight ahead as if Mom might not notice a tutu-wearing, green not-zombie the size of a four-year-old. I can see his chest moving up and down when he breathes. In fact, I think he might be hyperventilating.

"This?" I look at the Band-Aids as if they just showed up and surprised me. "Oh. No! I mean, yes! No. I have a sore toe, that's all."

"Let me see," Mom says, so I take off my sneaker and point to my big toe, and she coos over it and puts a Band-Aid on for me. When her head is down, I wave at Bob to get under the bed, but he's so busy pretending to be the world's weirdest stuffed animal that he doesn't even see me.

I'm trying to figure it out. Has she seen him? *Can* she see him?

A second later, I have my answer. Mom goes

straight to the bed, flips down the blanket, and tells me to get in. She doesn't even tell me to brush my teeth or anything. She says we need a little snuggle time, and when I'm in bed, practically squashed right up against Bob, she sits on the edge of the mattress and starts patting my head like she does sometimes.

She can't see him.

"I'm leaving early," Mom says. "Before breakfast. You'll probably still be asleep."

"Okay." I tell the stomachache not to show up, but it shows up anyway.

"You're good staying here with Gran, right? It'll be a lot more fun than all that time in the car."

"Sure." *Go away*, I tell the stomachache.

"She can't wait to have some real time with you, you know."

"I know."

"You're going to make that cake together, remember?"

"Yes."

Then Mom asks if I want a story. And of course, I do.

"Close your eyes," she says. "Once upon a time, there was a remarkably brave mouse named Leah." And she tells me about a mouse princess with a baby mouse sister who cries at exactly four p.m. every day, and there's a giant frog and a magic wishing well and a pie made out of flies and cheese. It's the kind of story she hasn't told me in a long time, the kind she used to tell me when I was little.

My stomach doesn't feel any better, but it doesn't feel worse, either.

"Did you make that up?" I ask when she gets to the *happily ever after* part.

She kisses my forehead. "It's my own silly version of an old fairy tale."

A fairy tale about a magic well?

Mom turns out the light, kisses me again, and whispers, "See you in a few days."

"Mom?"

"Yes?"

"You're not leaving until the morning, right?"

"Right." She blows me one more kiss and closes the door behind her.

"Did you hear that story?" I whisper to Bob when she's gone. "I wish *our* well were magic."

I feel him turn his head, and all I can see in the dark are his big wet eyes.

"I wish I had a mother," he says.

I don't know what to say. Bob is alone in the world. Totally, completely alone.

"Bob," I say finally. "Maybe you do have a mother. Maybe you have a whole big family!"

But he doesn't answer.

CHAPTER TEN

BOB

Are you ready?" Livy asks, standing by the door. She has a pink towel slung over her shoulder and a fresh bar of soap in her hand. She has decided I need a bath.

"It's been five years," I point out, arms crossed. "What's another few days?"

She makes a big show of pinching her nose closed.

"But what if I drown? We don't know if I can swim."

"You won't drown in the tub," she assures

me. "It's not even halfway full because of the drought."

"What if I slip down the drain? Maybe when a not-zombie gets wet all over he shrinks up into nothing?"

"I put the stopper in."

"Fine," I grumble, allowing her to lead me out of the room. "But I can't promise to use the soap."

"You'll use it all right," she says, pushing me ahead of her into the bathroom. She places the bar firmly into my hands and drapes the towel over the rim of the tub. I notice she has taken the liberty of filling the bathtub with a few inches of water. And bubbles. And is that . . . one of Gran's plastic roses floating on top?

"I thought your first bath in five years should be special," she says.

I roll my eyes but pull off the red sweatshirt and fold it carefully on the counter. I step

cautiously over to the tub. I wouldn't want to slip on a puddle and knock myself out.

"You're going to wear your tutu in the bathtub?"

I look down, half surprised to still be wearing it. I shrug. "I've grown accustomed to it." I dip one toe in the bubbly water. "It's warm!"

"What did you expect? It's a bath."

I had expected it to be cold, but I don't know why. I dip my toe again, then extend my foot out to Livy. "Does my toe look smaller to you?"

Livy groans. "Your toe does not look smaller. You are not shrinking."

It's true. I seem to be my same size.

"I'll be right outside, reading." She waves the book with the half knight, half person on the cover. "If Gran comes up I'll duck back in. Will you be okay alone?"

I nod.

"Don't forget to wash under your arms and behind your ears."

I roll my eyes.

"With soap!" she says before shutting the door behind her.

I double-check that the stopper is in place, then put my whole foot in the tub. Then the other. It feels . . . inviting. I slowly lower myself the rest of the way in, feeling the water cover my legs, then my belly, then my neck and arms. I lean back and feel myself relax.

"Ahhh, that feels nice." It does. It really does feel nice. But it's more than nice. It feels like . . . like home. Livy must have known the bath wasn't just about getting clean. She wanted to take both our minds off of last night. She doesn't know it, but her mother crept into our room early this morning and kissed her good-bye. I stood right in front of her mom and waved. It was dark in the room, but not *that* dark. She didn't see me at all.

I close my eyes to think. If Livy's mom doesn't see me at all, and a kid like Danny, who doesn't know me like Livy knows me, sees a chicken, then maybe age is another clue to my magic.

Baths are very good at helping one think.

I had lots of time to think in the closet, of course. I was alone, but I *wasn't* alone at the same time. I made a home for myself inside my head and I decorated it with all the things I learned and thought about and made with my Legos. I got in touch with my inner Bobness.

I know Livy feels awful about leaving me in there all those years, but after that admittedly rocky adjustment period, and once I taught myself to read, it was actually kind of awesome. My eyes pop open. I let her feel guilty when it wasn't even her fault. I never told her any of the good stuff!

I quickly scrub the places she told me to—and a few she left out. The bathwater is brown with dirt. Guess I did need a bath after all!

I climb out of the tub just as the doorbell rings. I stay quiet, clutching my towel and dripping water onto the rug. Livy was right, I should have taken off the tutu.

"Sarah!" Gran Nicholas says a few seconds later. "How lovely to see you! Come in, come in." I hear Livy stand up from her post outside the bathroom door and join Gran downstairs. Now Gran says, "Why don't you and Sarah catch up in your room for a while? You two used to giggle for hours."

Ugh. I need to talk to Livy RIGHT NOW and also I need to move my knight to f3 on my next turn instead of sacrificing my bishop as I was going to do. Baths are also good for chess strategizing.

"I actually only came by for my hoodie," Sarah says quickly. "I didn't mean to interrupt anything. It's just always cold at the restaurant."

Okay, I may not know a ton about human nature, but it sounds like the sweatshirt is just an excuse to see Livy.

"Don't be silly," Gran Nicholas says. "We're happy to have you, aren't we, Livy?"

"Sure," Livy says. "Your sweatshirt is up- stairs. I'll go get it."

But Gran insists there's plenty of time be- fore lunch and they should go up to play.

Super fast like the Flash, I grab the sweat-shirt from the counter, run to the bedroom, throw the sweatshirt on the bed, run into my closet, and close the door.

The girls come into the room. Livy is talking REALLY LOUDLY to warn me she's not alone, but she forgets I have super hearing. Or maybe I never told her.

While they get settled I struggle to put on the chicken suit, which has shrunk at least two sizes. I pull on the neck to try to stretch it out, but it doesn't help much.

"You still have Rufus!" Sarah exclaims.

I put my eye up to the crack in the door-frame. She is taller than Livy, with yellow hair, and she is hugging Rufus. *My* Rufus. Well, not mine exactly, but more mine than *this* girl's.

I recognize her even though she got a lot big-ger. After Old Livy left, this girl used to come up to read the books on the bookshelf a few times. She even took one once. I saw her tuck it under her jacket. She stops by to see Gran now and again with her family, but for the past few years she's only been a voice downstairs. And now she's here at a really bad time and I wish she'd leave.

"You know Rufus?" Livy asks her.

Sarah nods.

Gran Nicholas comes in with a tray of cookies and sets it down on the dresser. "Are you two getting reacquainted?"

The girls don't answer. I don't think they know what *reacquainted* means. I do, though, because the *R*s had a lot of good words. It means getting to know each other again. I've had a lot of personal experience with that lately.

"I also brought you this." Gran Nicholas hands Livy something small and rectangular, but I can't tell what it is.

"Your tape recorder?" Livy asks.

"Don't be so surprised. You girls used to record yourselves singing into it."

Livy reddens. "I have such a bad voice."

"That's not what I remember," Gran says.

Sarah takes the tape recorder and presses a button. A few seconds later the unmistakable sound of two five-year-old girls singing a pop song fills the air. Even though I'm annoyed at having to wait like this, I can't help but smile. They sound so happy and carefree. Livy sounds like the old Livy. The one who didn't care if her singing voice wasn't the best in the world.

"That's embarrassing," Livy says, reaching over and switching it off.

"Totally," Sarah says.

"I think it's lovely," Gran says, leaving the room. "You two have fun."

Livy grabs a cookie. "Sorry about taking your sweatshirt home."

"That's okay," Sarah says. I hear the bed squeak as she sits down. "I didn't really come here for the hoodie."

I *knew* it!

CHAPTER ELEVEN

LIVY

You didn't?" I ask Sarah.

She shakes her head. "I wanted to see you. And I kind of wanted to see if you still had Violet and Abigail."

"Who?"

Sarah points to the other side of the bed, where there are two dolls sitting up on the bedside table. I haven't even really looked at them before.

"I think those are my mom's old dolls," I say. And I get this pang. My brain still hasn't forgotten about trying to sleep here without Mom in the house tonight.

Sarah nods. "You were Violet. I was Abigail."

"Really? Did we play with dolls last time? That's hilarious."

"Why hilarious?"

"Oh, not hilarious—I just mean, you know: I haven't touched a doll in like three years."

"I like dolls," Sarah says. "Sometimes."

"Really? But you're—"

"I'm what?"

"Um, you just seem kind of grown-up. You sort of have a job, even."

"Not 'sort of.' I do have a job," Sarah says. "Every Friday night and every Sunday afternoon, at Mom's restaurant. It's fun when I'm in the mood. Which is definitely not every Friday night and Sunday afternoon."

"So—they make you?"

"It's not like that. We all help out. You know,

do what we can. Even Danny does stuff to help."

"What can he do? He's only seven, right?"

"He's pretty good at setting the tables before the restaurant opens—he knows where everything goes." Sarah glances at Mom's dolls again and says, "Confession. I come over here sometimes."

"Why?"

She shrugs. "To talk to your gran. To look at your mom's books." She smiles. "And to get away from Danny. I know you always wanted to be a big sister, but trust me, it can be annoying."

I always wanted to be a big sister?

"And now you are one, which is cool. I know your baby sister can't do much yet. But soon she'll follow you everywhere."

"Everywhere? Even to the bathroom?"

Sarah nods and then makes a face. "*Everywhere*. So sometimes I used to come over here

and pretend this was my room, and my bed, and my books. . . ."

"And your dolls?"

She looks at them again.

"Have you ever played truth or dare?" I ask her.

She shakes her head.

"I'll teach you."

Truth or dare is simple: You either do the dare or you have to answer one question, and you have to answer it honestly. I start off easy, daring Sarah to go down to the kitchen and bring something back without saying one word to Gran, even if she's standing right there.

Sarah nods and marches off. As soon as she's gone, I run to the closet to check on Bob.

"When is she *leaving*?" Bob asks. "I have something to tell you."

"Soon," I say. He's wearing what's left of the chicken suit. It's tight.

He huffs a little. "How soon?"

"Do you know her?" I ask. "She says she hung out in here sometimes."

He nods. "Sometimes she came and looked at the dolls. Once she almost opened the closet! I hope you're not thinking of playing chess with her, because I have a really good move. That's *our* game. Oh great, here she comes!" He pulls the closet door closed one second before Sarah walks in holding an egg.

"My turn!" she says.

I casually turn my back to the closet as if there isn't a jealous green mysterious creature inside. "Okay. I pick . . . dare."

"And you have to do whatever I dare you to do? Or answer one question with the absolute truth? Is that right?"

I tell her yes, that's exactly right.

And then Sarah dares me to drink a raw egg.

"Are you sure that you haven't played this game before?" I ask suspiciously. "You seem very good at it." Because this is exactly the kind of dare I would come up with if I really wanted to make someone choose truth.

"I'm a fast learner," she says, holding up the egg. "So are you going to drink it? I could get you a cup."

I shake my head. "I'll take truth."

Sarah smiles, throwing herself onto the middle of the bed. She leans over to grab Abigail and Violet, and then gets up on her knees, holding up one doll in each hand. "Here's my question: Do you *really* not like playing with dolls anymore? Or do you just think you're too *cool* to play with dolls?"

She kind of sticks her hip out when she says *cool*, but she's still smiling, and suddenly I like Sarah. I walk over and say, "Which one is Violet again?"

She waggles the one wearing the blue dress. I take it from her and push Violet's black yarn hair out of her cloth face. Her dress is nice, actually. It's got puff sleeves and a shiny purple sash. "Okay, fine," I say. "Dolls are sort of fun."

"I knew it!" Sarah hugs Abigail to her chest and says, "Let's forget truth or dare. Let's have a dance party with Abigail and Violet!" She hops off the bed and presses play on the tape recorder, which is still lying on the floor, and our screechy five-year-old voices start spilling out of it again.

She grabs Abigail's hands and starts dancing her around at the foot of the bed, looking totally ridiculous. So I hold Violet's tiny little hands and start doing the tango. It's this crazy old dance my dad showed me once. When the horrible singing finally stops, we fall down on the rug, breathing hard. It's kind of great. I wonder if Sarah might be the kind of friend I can talk to. At home, some of my friends are like that. But not all of them. I thought Maya was like that, until she told Audrey how my dad had to come and pick me up because I was too scared to sleep over.

There's a clicking sound from the tape recorder, which I guess we left running. And then I hear my voice, alone, saying:

"This is a story for when you're lonely, Bob. It's called, um . . . 'The Cow and the Pig.' One day a dog named Tucker was walking down the road . . ."

I slam my hand down on top of it, hitting all the buttons at once. My voice stops.

"That was so cute!" Sarah says. "A story about a dog called 'The Cow and the Pig'!"

"Yeah, ha!" I say. "Funny."

"Who's Bob?" she asks, sticking a cookie in her mouth. "You asked about him before. There's no Bob around here."

When I can't think of what to say, she says, "Maybe Bob was your invisible friend."

"I . . . had an invisible friend?"

She flops back on the rug and says, "Sure, we both did. Mine was called Philippa."

I hear a little noise from inside the closet

behind me and quickly move my foot so it might seem like I just kicked the door by accident.

"You remember a lot about when I was here before," I tell Sarah.

"Well, we don't get a lot of visitors. Hey, speaking of your invisible friend, have you dug up your time capsule yet?"

"My what?"

"Your time capsule! That's what you called it. You said you were going to bury it before you went back home."

This feels important. "Do you happen to remember where I buried it?"

She smiles. "Sorry. I can't remember things I never knew. You said it was for your invisible friend. Maybe you should ask *him*."

And then she laughs.

CHAPTER TWELVE

BOB

Livy laughs, too, but only for a second. Then she asks, all casual-like, "Is Philippa still around?"

My little green heart is beating so fast (at least I *think* my heart is green). AM I AN INVISIBLE FRIEND? Is *that* what I am? No superpowers or magic? Is that why Livy's mom couldn't see me? And perhaps most importantly, IS THERE SOMEONE ELSE LIKE ME? I hold my breath until Sarah answers.

"Not anymore, of course."

Instead of being disappointed, my heart quickens even more. Does that mean Sarah's invisible friend found her way home? Maybe Sarah knows how to get ME home, too. *Ask her,* I want to shout to Livy. *Ask her how she got Philippa home.*

"Oh," Livy says quickly. "I mean, duh, of course." She grabs a cookie from the plate. I can tell she's not going to let this drop. Still making it sound like no big deal, she asks, "So, what kinds of things did you guys do together? Philippa, I mean."

Sarah reaches for another cookie, too. At the rate they are chomping through these cookies the hope of any being left over for me is shrinking. I am amazed that I can still think of snacks at an important moment like this, but there you have it.

"Well, one time you came over and we all had a tea party."

Livy stops chewing. "I brought my invisible friend over to your house for a tea party?"

Sarah shakes her head. "No, it was only the three of us. You said yours wouldn't want to get dressed up and pretend to drink from little cups."

I have to smile. Livy always looked out for me.

"Though I bet he'd look pretty cute in a tutu," Livy says rather loudly. Clearly she knows I'm eavesdropping.

"If you say so," Sarah says, then adds, "I haven't thought about Philippa in years."

"What happened to her? At the end, I mean."

I know Livy's face so well that even though her back is to me I know she's holding her breath right now. This is it! This is when I find out how I'll get home! I press my eye right up to the crack and hold my breath, too.

Sarah shrugs. "I got bored of pretending to see her, I guess."

"Oh," Livy says. It's a sad *oh*. Sarah's invisible friend wasn't real. Not in the same way I'm real. I feel foolish and slump down to the floor. Unfortunately I land squarely on the mast of the pirate ship and then jump back up with Legos sticking where Legos shouldn't stick. I must have made a noise, because both girls turn to face the closet.

Livy jumps up. "Thanks for coming today, it was fun. I'm still kinda jet-lagged though, so I think I'm gonna take a nap."

"Okay," Sarah says, standing up from the rug.

Livy looks all around the room and grabs one of those creepy dolls. "Do you want to borrow Abigail? I'm sure my mom won't mind."

"No thanks," Sarah says. And I think she's finally going to leave, because one hand is on the doorknob, but then she says, "Do you want to hang out later?"

"I can't," Livy says. "I'm making a cake with my grandmother now that the baby is out of the house."

Then they leave to walk downstairs and I

come out of my closet and sit on the edge of the bed. Only crumbs are left on the cookie tray.

Why am I not surprised?

Livy comes back in and closes the door and flops on the bed. "I think you need a larger chicken suit. That one's like, five times too small for you now." Before I can argue that no one taught me proper laundry techniques, she reaches under the pillow and pulls out a cookie. "Saved you one."

I lean past the cookie and reach around and hug her bony shoulders.

"You smell clean, but what was that for?" she asks when I finally let go.

"For the cookie. For not making me go to a tea party. For tape-recording stories for me to listen to even though I never got them."

"Guess you saw the dancing," she says.

"You've got some good moves."

She smiles. "I do, don't I?"

"You don't need to feel bad about leaving

me in the closet," I blurt out, then take a bite of the cookie. I chomp and talk and crumbs fly out as I try to explain how I was never alone because I had my imagination to keep me company.

Man, this cookie tastes good!

When I finally run out of words, she says, "Didn't anyone tell you not to talk with your mouth full? All I heard between crunches was something about you exploring your inner Bob."

I swallow my last bite. "That's pretty much the gist of it."

"You have a Lego stuck to your leg," she says, reaching over to pluck it off. "You really didn't get tired of building that same ship over and over?"

I smile. "In between I'd make whatever word I was reading in the dictionary. The aardvark was my first. I was particularly proud of that one."

She tilts her head at me. "How many

different objects can you make from one pirate ship?"

"Exactly three thousand and nine. So far."

She nods, clearly impressed. It *is* impressive.

"So it was a ship but also all those other things."

"Yes."

She tosses the Lego piece back into the closet and grabs her shoes.

"Where are you going?" I ask.

"*We* are going to search the farm for that time capsule Sarah talked about. One thing can be lots of other things, right? So a time capsule can also be a clue. Who knows what I put in there. It could take a while to find it, so bring a flashlight."

My spirits rise and rise. We're going on an adventure! "We don't need to bring one," I tell her with a grin.

"Why not?"

"Because I know exactly where you buried it."

CHAPTER THIRTEEN

LIVY

I distract Gran by asking for a snack while Bob slips out the back door. We're supposed to meet under the farthest tree in the yard, near our Sylvester rock. I find him relaxing against the tree trunk with his eyes closed and his legs straight out in front of him.

"You look happy," I tell him. I hand him half a slice of banana bread and kneel beside the rock to get to work, feeling around its edges. It's a *big* rock. How are we going to get under this thing? How could I have hidden something under it when I was five?

"I *am* happy," Bob says cheerfully. "We're together, aren't we? We're outside! And we're looking for clues. We're going to find my mother. Like you said, my large family! So I won't be lonely when you leave again." He smiles into the sun. "Plus, I have ba-nana bread! It's like a banana, with bread!"

I glance at him as I

try to scrape the dirt out from under one side of the rock. It gets under my nails and up my nose. "Don't get your hopes up, okay, Bob?"

He blinks at me. "Why not? *Old* Livy never told me not to get my hopes up."

"I'm just . . . being careful. Of your feelings. Okay? We don't know for sure that we'll find anything here."

"Oh, we will," Bob says. "We will find whatever the old Livy hid underneath the Sylvester rock! For me, her invisible friend."

Bob is one hundred percent sure that the old Livy hid the invisible-friend time capsule under the Sylvester rock. He says that for the last two days she was at Gran's, Old Livy got a "certain look" on her face whenever we got near this rock.

"*That's* how you know?" I asked him. "My expression? Five years ago?"

Bob nodded. "Oh yes. Whenever we came close to this rock, Old Livy's face said, 'I've got a secret.' It was loud and clear."

I know it sounds ridiculous, but it's worth a try. We have to start looking somewhere. And I have to admit that Bob is pretty good at reading faces. Especially mine.

So I'm scratching the hard-packed dirt away from the sides of the rock, trying to find any gaps where I might have hidden something.

Now I'm pretty much coated in dirt-dust. I sneeze.

I look over at Bob. His eyes are closed.

"Hey! Why are you just sitting there?"

"I'm not just sitting here! I'm feeling the sun on my face. And I'm also being careful of you."

I sit back on my heels and try to slap some of the dirt off my hands. It makes a big dust cloud that makes me sneeze *again*. "Careful of me? What are you talking about?"

He gets a patient look on his face. I'm pretty good at reading Bob's face, too, I realize. "I am being careful of your fingers, Livy. You are playing very near the rock, and I don't want to drop it on you when I pick it up." He smiles and closes his eyes again. "Just tell me when you're done playing in the dirt. I'm not in a hurry. I'm just enjoying the outdoors."

I stand up. "Bob, I'm not playing, I'm *working*. And we can't 'pick up' this rock. This rock is *huge*. First, we're going to dig out some of the dirt underneath and then we'll both get on one side and we'll try to tilt—"

I stop talking.

Bob has picked up the rock and is holding it over his head. "Where should I put it?" he asks. "If you're done playing?"

Speechless, I point to the tree he was leaning against, and he carefully props the rock against the tree trunk.

"Bob," I say. "You're—*strong*."

He nods. "Yes."

"How did you—Look!" Because there is something lying in a little dug-out place in the dirt, almost exactly where I had just been digging. There must have been a little hollow spot under one edge of the rock. But five years later, it's packed hard with dirt.

"You were right, Bob!" I brush the dirt off the top of whatever it is and pick it up. It's a glass jar, sealed with a metal lid.

Bob doesn't even look surprised. He just gently puts the Sylvester rock back into place, as casually as Superman would.

I try the lid, but it won't turn.

Bob takes the jar from me, but says, "Let's open it at Gran's, after you wash your hands. This is Old Livy's treasure, and I don't want to get it dirty."

Bob does his best chicken walk all the way back to the house. It doesn't seem to matter that chickens can't really hold things.

CHAPTER FOURTEEN

BOB

Gran is on the phone in the den and we slip right past her and up the stairs. Her voice is crackly and high-pitchy, which means she's talking to the bank again.

After I supervise her handwashing, Livy gets to work twisting off the lid. She grunts. She groans. I try to keep still but it is not easy. Finally she lowers her arms. "This is on good! I must have been stronger when I was five."

"You were different strong," I tell her, holding out my palm. She places the jar in my hand and I only have to twist the tiniest bit and the lid pops off.

"I'm sure you loosened it up," I tell her, handing it back.

"Uh-huh." She peeks in, then turns it over. It takes a few forceful shakes before three things fall out onto the bed—two pieces of black licorice and a rolled-up photograph of Old Livy sitting on the floor in front of the bookshelf in this very room, reading a book upside down. The book is upside down, that is. Livy herself is right side up.

And that's it. I look at her and she looks at me.

"I'd have thought a time capsule would contain more stuff," I say, grabbing a piece of the licorice.

"You're not really gonna eat that, right? It's five years old!"

I pop it in my mouth. "Stale licorice is better than no licorice any day." Livy's hand darts out and grabs the second piece before I can get it.

"Let's make sure you survive the first one," she says, sticking it in her pocket. She picks up the photograph.

"Why would I have put this one picture in there?" she wonders out loud. I'm kind of insulted there's nothing about me in the jar. Would it have been so hard to put in a feather from my chicken suit?

She picks up the photo, then flips it over. "Hey, Bob. Look! Something's glued onto the back." She peels it off and holds it up with a grin. "It's a feather from your chicken suit!"

I smile sheepishly, ashamed of myself. Of course Livy wouldn't have left me out. I take the feather and stick it onto one of the many bare spots on my belly. It's in much better condition than all the rest.

"The picture is pretty cute," I tell her, looking closer. Old Livy is obviously pretending to

read the oversized book. It looks like a cool book, with lots of colorful pictures on both covers. I twist my head until I can read the title. *"Fairy and Folk Tales from A to Z."* It's like my dictionary! *A* to *Z*! I don't think I know any fairy or folk tales, but Livy does, or at least her mother does.

Livy studies the picture, too. Suddenly she grabs my arm. "Bob! Who does that look like on the cover?" She stabs her finger at the picture.

"What do you mean?" I turn it so the book cover is facing the right way and try to identify the objects from the cover. "Is that a mermaid?"

"Yes," she says impatiently. "It's a mermaid on a rock, a three-headed lion, a lumberjack, a fairy, and you!"

"Me!" I grab the photo back. The only drawing on the cover I don't recognize as one of those other things is some kind of short green creature with one eyebrow. Okay, I see why she'd think I bear a slight resemblance to the creature in the drawing, but no. I shake my head. "I think you just insulted the character in the book. He's much more handsome than me."

"Bob," she says. "You look EXACTLY like this guy." She pushes me out the door of the bedroom and into the bathroom and makes me face the mirror. I take a step back. I've never really looked at myself before! I turn this way and that, admiring my reflection from all angles.

"I'm not half bad!"

I keep preening because it's making her laugh. Then she stops. "Seriously, though. This book must tell us what you are. It's been here all along! C'mon!" She races back to her room and I hurry after. The phone rings and I hear Gran answer it downstairs. Maybe the bank is calling back.

"It's got to be here somewhere," Livy is saying, pulling books off the shelves with both hands.

It's not on the shelves.

"Maybe it's under the bed," she says. She throws back the covers and ducks down and spreads her arms out like she's swimming.

It's not under the bed.

"Where else could it be?" she asks, throwing up her hands.

I think about it, and it hits me that I know exactly where it is! "Livy, the book is at—"

But before I can tell her that Sarah took it after Livy went back home last time, Gran shouts upstairs. "Livy! Please come down right away. I need you!" She sounds more urgent than I've ever heard her, even more worked up than the time a woman from the bank came all the way to the house.

Livy looks torn, but only for a second. She says, "I'll be right back—keep looking." I open my mouth, but she's already flying down the stairs. I sit on the bed and wait. That's where I am when the front door slams and Gran's car drives away. With Livy in it!

Well that stinks.

I move to the top of the stairs and listen to all the silence, my chest tight and my head swimmy. This is a familiar feeling. I call it the Feeling of Livy Leaving Suddenly Without Telling Me When or If She's Coming Back. I know this feeling well.

I stand up from the stairs. Livy's not gone for good. I know that this time. No more feeling sorry for myself and waiting. I have a book with a strikingly handsome green creature on the cover to find, and there's no time to waste.

I straighten my head comb and use the tape on the desk in the corner of the kitchen to secure a few feathers that are hanging loose. I grab two pickles and a loaf of bread, eat one pickle and two slices of bread with butter. Then I continue my rushing out.

I am a not-zombie fake chicken on a mission!

CHAPTER FIFTEEN

LIVY

Sarah's restaurant is full of worried people and worried voices. A man and a woman stand together over a table, sketching and labeling maps on paper tablecloths: Everett's Paddock, the bush behind Callen's Place, Horse Paddock East, Horse Paddock West. And underneath they're writing people's names. I look around for Sarah, her mom or her grandpa, but they aren't here. I don't know anyone here. I squeeze the pawn in my hand and tell myself, *Bob. Don't forget Bob.*

I didn't even have a chance to tell him where we were going. When I ran downstairs, Gran was hanging up her yellow kitchen phone.

She said, "Get your shoes on, honey."

"I'm wearing them," I said, pointing to my sandals.

"No—your sneakers."

By the time I found them, Gran was already out the door, and I had to run to catch up.

"Danny is missing," she told me, starting the car. "He never came home for lunch. Don't worry yet—" She tried to give me a quick smile. "He does this from time to time. But the town is organizing a search."

Gran and I are at the restaurant to help. "This is Sarah's aunt Diedre," Gran says quickly. "And her husband, Malcolm." She turns to them. "What can we do?"

Diedre scans the paper. "You okay with walking the northeast quadrant of the bush behind Callen's Place?" She points to one of her sketches. "From the sheep fence up to the road? I know it's a lot, but there's so much ground to cover."

"Of course," Gran says. "We'll go right now."

Malcolm presses a little paper bag into Gran's hand and another one into mine. "The restaurant's telephone number is in there in case you have something to tell us, and some snacks and water. It's hot. Don't forget to hydrate."

Gran nods and feels for my hand without looking at me, and then we are out the door and into the sunlight again.

CHAPTER SIXTEEN

BOB

I peck and side-step my way down the dirt road that leads from Gran's farmhouse to Sarah's farmhouse next door. If her grandpa is home with the little boy it will be harder to sneak in, but I have fooled them before, so my confidence is high. Well, high-*ish*.

Three cars and a tractor pass me on the road and I cough from the dirt their wheels send up. I leap into the tall, brown grass on the side of the road each time I hear one coming. Now I am dirty and scratched up by the pointy grass. I do not look my best.

I've never been this far from the house before. It's scary but kind of exciting, too. I'm like the great explorers of the old days, setting out on new adventures, discovering faraway lands.

Except I can still see Livy's bedroom window from here.

I must say, I have excellent eyesight.

I peck and side-step a few more minutes, but it's slow going this way. I decide to run because chickens can run. I am not even out of breath when I reach the farmhouse. Not to brag, it's just a fact. I am learning all sorts of things about myself on this journey already!

The farmhouse is bigger than Gran's, but the wood is painted a lime green that I find a bit off-putting. Some of the grass in the front yard is scorched. They must have had a small fire. Gran's always worrying about fires in the bush during a long drought like this one. I guess it can happen on farms, too. Scary. The house seems fine, though.

I crouch in the tall grass across the street,

and with my really good vision I scope out the place. One should always scope out one's surroundings before sneaking in. Gran watches a lot of detective shows, so I know a lot about stakeouts.

This is what I see:

Driveway: one brown truck, one white car with a thick blue stripe down the side. The white car is very dirty. White is not a sensible color in hot, dusty environments.

Front lawn: a folding table with a round-shaped bald man in a folding chair behind it. The man wears a blue outfit with a badge on his chest and is handing a map to a lady and two boys a few years younger than Livy, both in shorts and round hats that are too big for them.

The man in blue is a policeman. Why is a policeman sitting outside Sarah's house? He is not selling lemonade. I shrink farther back into the bush and peek out between the reeds. I don't want to be spotted by the long arm of the law.

When I am certain there is no one else around, I sneak up the driveway, being sure to keep on the far side of the parked cars. The policeman doesn't even look up from his notebook. I'm THAT good.

I keep going around the side of the house, past the chickens in their coop. They cluck and eye me suspiciously. I am unliked by chickens everywhere. They don't seem convinced that I am one of them. In my current sorry state, I don't blame them.

The fields of Sarah's house are in even worse condition than Gran's. Most of the ground is bare, with only a few wilted sunflowers here and there.

I hurry past a sad-looking cow who is too busy flicking flies away from her ears to pay me any attention. Their kitchen door is where ours is, so I expect it to be unlocked, like ours is. But when I reach up to turn the knob, I discover my luck has run out. Then I notice the square cut out of the bottom of the door. A thin plastic flap hangs in front with a picture of a dog bone printed on it. I am going to have to crawl through a door clearly made for a dog. This is not one of my finer moments. I am glad Livy is not here to watch.

I suck in my belly and wiggle headfirst through the hole and onto the hard kitchen floor. At least there's no dog snarling down at me. I use the shiny surface of the oven to adjust my chicken outfit and to dust off the worst of the patches of dirt I've brought in with me.

The kitchen looks like someone left in a big hurry. Cabinets hang open and a half-eaten meal sits out on the table. I can hear the policeman outside talking on the phone, so there's no time to spare. Still, I do manage to finish a cheese sandwich that only had one bite taken out of it. Keeping up one's strength is very important when on a mission like this, and I will need enough energy to make it back to our house.

May as well take the ham slice, too.

I wash down the ham with a glass of milk as I bound up the stairs two at a time. I find Sarah's room easily because of the red sweatshirt in the middle of the floor. Also, it says SARAH'S ROOM in multicolored letters on the door. I open drawers and push aside the clothes hanging in her wardrobe, spotting other books, but not the right one. I feel slightly guilty for invading her privacy, but this wouldn't be necessary if she'd just returned the book when she was finished with it.

I sit on the floor and lean against the back of the bed and think. If it's not here, then where? I stare out into the hallway, and my eyes wander across the hall to Sarah's little brother's room. I jump up.

Danny!

He had a book with him that day at the well! I wasn't paying close attention at the time, but there were definitely a collection of drawings decorating the cover. And it was a big book, just like the one in the photograph! He could have taken it from Sarah's room, or maybe Sarah had meant to return it to Livy and he found it.

Or I could be totally wrong and it was a different book with him at Gran's well and Sarah lost the fairy-tale book years ago or returned it to the public library by mistake. Gran did that once. I heard her on the phone trying to get it back.

His room is even messier than his sister's. Frankly, I'm surprised their mother lets them get away with this. I repeat the lifting and opening and looking under things. Then I glance up at the wall above the bed and see something that stops me in my tracks.

It's a painting of a well, like the one in Gran's yard, only this one has a trickling creek running past it and a weird tree beside it, and it's made of brick instead of stone. I climb on the bed and stand in front of the picture to get a better look. The paint is still slightly wet in places.

Other than the wonky tree, I can't see anything too special about the painting. But just as I'm about to hop off to continue my search for the book, I spot a detail that makes me lean so close to the painting that my nose comes away with a dab of blue sky on it.

On the far side of the well, *something* is climbing out. Something with four long, green fingers that grip the side of the brick wall.

A shiver and a kind of numb feeling begins in my face and extends down to my toes when I spot the small words painted across the bottom of the well.

PLEASE HELP US, WELL DWELLERS

CHAPTER SEVENTEEN

LIVY

Gran and I have a rule for the bush (which is what Australians call the woods): We have to be close enough to see each other. We're walking along a dirt path that she tells me used to be a creek bed. She tells me to watch where I put my feet. She doesn't say so, but I'm pretty sure it's because of snakes. I have a whistle in my jeans pocket "just in case we get separated," and also to blow once in a while in case Danny can hear it.

I also have a system Gran doesn't know

anything about. My black pawn is in the same pocket as my whistle. So every time I blow the whistle, I feel the pawn and think, *Bob*. I can't stand the thought of forgetting him again.

"Do you think Danny's okay?" I ask Gran.

She nods. "Danny's an explorer. He knows the bush around here. It's been his nature to wander ever since he could walk upright. The problem is that he isn't so great about keeping track of the time. Blow that whistle again, will you?"

I blow my whistle as hard as I can.

We listen, in case Danny is calling back to us. Nothing.

"Was my mom like that too when she was little? A wanderer?"

Gran shook her head. "She wasn't much of a bush wanderer. More of a traveler, if you know what I mean. Good head on her shoulders from the beginning. A pleasure to spend time with. I just wish I got to spend more of mine with her. And with you."

Gran is alone, too. I don't know why I never thought of it before. I think of the last five years, and Gran and Bob living in the same house all that time. I can't decide if it's nice or just really sad.

"Why don't you move to America? You could live at our house! I'm sure Mom and Dad wouldn't mind."

Gran nods. "They've offered. Problem is, I love it here." She raises her arms and kind of waves at the trees. "I love the place and I love the people."

So maybe it's not sad that Gran lives alone. Maybe it's a choice.

"But what if it never rains again here?" I ask her.

She makes a quick face—like a face she might make if I were blowing that whistle right in her ear. Then she says, "I guess I'll have to take that question one day at a time."

I'm not sure what to say to that. Because

what if it *really* never rains here again? Gran catches my hand and we swing our arms back and forth together. It feels good. Then she says, "So you're feeling okay about staying over tonight?"

Mom has obviously told her about my sleepover problems. "Yeah. I think so." I wait. No stomachache. Small twinge-y feeling, but no stomachache.

She squeezes my hand. "Good. You know what your mom used to do when she couldn't sleep? She put a book under her pillow."

"She never told me that."

Gran smiles. "She said it helped her dream."

I picture that: Mom, my age, in the four-poster bed, dreaming. It feels good.

"Blow that whistle again," Gran says.

I blow. We listen. No Danny.

Then Gran says, "You were quite a wanderer yourself when you were here last."

"Me?"

"Yes, you!" she says. "You know it was just you and me for a few days last time you came, right? Your mom was away seeing friends, just like she is now. Well, one morning I come downstairs at six a.m. and there you are sitting at the breakfast table in your pajamas, big innocent smile on your face. You had even set the table! Knife, fork, and cup for you; knife, fork, and cup for me. Only problem was that your pajamas looked like you'd been out in the bush all night in the rain—leaves and dirt and anything else you can think of that you might find on the ground. Everywhere. Your pockets were full of it. And you were *wet*."

I have a pretty good idea which morning this was. "Gran, how do you think I got wet?"

She shakes her head. "Livy, to this day I have no earthly idea how you got wet, and believe me when I say I've put serious thought into it. I thought, maybe the pig trough? But no, that gate was latched, way up high. I checked. The whole episode scared the heck out of me, actually. After that I started waking myself up at four a.m. to watch the doors."

"Wow," I say. "That's weird." It probably wouldn't be a big comfort to her to know that I'm ninety-nine percent sure I fell into her well.

Gran says, "Blow that whistle again, Livy."

I blow. We listen. No Danny.

"Gran, do you remember a book with a mermaid on the cover? And—some other stuff?"

We're walking uphill now, and she's breathing hard. "Your big book, you mean?"

"What do you mean, my big book?"

"That's what you called it—your big book. I think it was called *The Big Book of Fairy Tales.* Something like that. It was your mother's, when she was a girl. I used to read it to her, but you never let me read it to you." She smiles.

"Why not?"

"You said you liked to make your *own* stories. You couldn't read a word, but you looked at that book a lot. I guess you liked the pictures."

"What kind of pictures?"

"Well, mermaids, like you said." She's still a little bit out of breath.

"Anything else?"

"Oh, sure. Elves, maybe? Fairies? I'm sorry, sweetie. I haven't seen that one in a while." Gran's distracted, looking at her ripped paper-tablecloth map. "We should turn left soon. There's a big rock about a quarter mile ahead. We'll turn right after that."

We walk on. The hill gets steeper. I scan the woods. No Danny. I climb up on a fallen tree trunk and turn around in a circle, looking. I blow my whistle, two toots. I hear a few answer-whistles from the other searchers—two toots. But no Danny. I'm about to climb down when I see a flash of orange. A very familiar shade of orange. Bob! I glance around—where did he go?

I squeeze my pawn. Scan, turn, scan—

Then I see it—one skinny green arm, waving at me, semi-desperately. He's right beside the path a little way ahead of us. But Gran is slowing down.

"Gran. Let's keep going."

"Actually, my dear, I think I need to sit down for a few minutes."

CHAPTER EIGHTEEN

BOB

"Did anyone else just see a chicken shimmy down that drainpipe?" one of the big-hatted boys had shouted. "It had something rolled up under its wing!"

"Maybe it was a wombat," his friend (or brother) had suggested.

"This was no wombat!"

The woman with them swatted them on the heads and said not to tell tales.

It was epic.

I wait for Livy to join me behind the tree.

"Wait till you hear what I've learned!" I say when she finally arrives, huffing and puffing. She puts up a *give me a minute* finger. Then she takes out a whistle and blows hard into it. Twice.

I put my hands over my ears. "Ouch! Finely tuned sense of sound, remember?"

"Sorry. I have to blow it every two minutes." We hear two more whistle blows, close by but less painful. Livy smiles. "That's Gran. She's resting." She twists around, likely making sure we're alone, before asking, "What are you doing here, Bob?"

"After you left me without saying anything even though you know I'm sensitive about that . . ." I pause as she reaches out to pat me on the head, a gesture I choose to interpret as an apology. Then I continue. "I decided to make myself useful." I take a deep breath and try to untangle all my thoughts before continuing. "I remembered that Sarah had taken the book from your mom's shelf and I went to get it back. And look!" I hold up the picture I took off the wall. The painting is a little smudged by my nose pressing against it, but only a little. "Look at that hand!"

She grabs it. "Where did you get this?"

"From over Danny's bed. He must have made it after reading the story!"

She leans in so close her nose comes away with a spot of blue, too!

"And what do you think *well dweller* means? I still haven't gotten up to the *W*s in my dictionary yet."

When she looks at me her eyes are shining. "Bob, I don't think it's in the dictionary. But this is it! The final clue we were looking for! You came out of Gran's well. You did! Rufus fell in, and I fell in, and you were there to save us!"

I frown. "But I don't feel like I came from a well. And visiting it yesterday didn't bring back any memories."

"I know, but maybe that's part of how your magic protects you or something."

"Protects me by making me forget where I came from? What kind of second-rate magic is that?"

"It's not the best," Livy agrees. "I bet the book would tell us more."

"Yes! Let's go ask Danny where it is."

She frowns. "No one is sure where Danny is right now. I should have told you that right away. That's why Gran took me. There's a big search on for him."

That would explain all the commotion and the policeman! "What are we waiting for then? Let's go find him!"

"I know! I'm trying!" She turns back to the painting. "Maybe we could use this painting as a map. He could be at this very well right now! Look, there's a weird tree near it like this." She holds out her arms and makes them all crooked and tilts her head. "And there's a creek bed leading up to it, too, just like the one we're standing on."

I look down. The dirt-filled creek is only about an inch or two lower than the ground on either side of it. We'd been using it like a path through the trees. "Livy, if neither of us passed the tree on our way here, it has to still be up ahead."

We take off running along the path, heading deeper and deeper into the bush. Livy continues blowing that awful whistle every two minutes, making me jump even though I know it's coming. Gran's responses are getting fainter as we get farther away. We'll have to find the well soon or else go back before Gran gets too worried and people start searching for *us*.

We step over broken twigs and bits of bark and I'm glad my feet are thick. Seedpods keep cracking and making us jump, thinking it's the sound of a fire starting. Finally we stumble into a small clearing and Livy grabs my arm and points. "It's the weird tree!"

She's right! And behind the tree, almost completely hidden by its long, oddly shaped branches and surprisingly green leaves, is a large brick well. My heart thumps with anticipation.

The first thing that I notice as we approach is the complete lack of a green hand gripping the edge of the well, or signs of any hands at all—green or Danny-sized. My shoulders sag. Were we wrong about everything? Was the drawing just a picture Danny made when he was bored?

She shuffles one way around the well, and I go the other. At the same time, we shout, "Danny!"

Because here he is, leaning against the back of the well, the missing book open on his lap. He sees us and points to a cardboard box on the ground beside him.

"No one came to take it."

CHAPTER NINETEEN
LIVY

When Danny stands up, I grab his hand like he might run somewhere. "Are you okay? A lot of people are looking for you."

The well seems to smother my words. It feels different from Gran's well. Like this might be the deepest, quietest place in the world. I step up to the well wall and peer into the murky darkness.

"Again?" Danny pulls his hand away. "I know my way home."

Then I notice Bob, who seems torn between

the box on the ground and the book in Danny's hand.

The book in his hand! He's holding the book with Bob on the cover!

"I think there might be a cupcake inside that box," Bob whispers to me.

But I'm a lot more interested in the book.

"Can I see the story?" I ask Danny. He knows the one I mean. He hands over the book.

"It's not true anyway," Danny says as I read down the table of contents. "There are only two wells around here. The one in your gran's yard and this abandoned one. I've waited and waited at both of them, and they never come. It's all a lie."

The story titled "The Well Dwellers" is only two pages long. I hold the book open, and Bob jumps in front of me.

I skim: *Well dwellers possess a secret and powerful magic. They can make things grow. They live all over the world in secret—*

"Bob," I say, "move your head—I can't see!"

Danny is staring. "Your chicken is named Bob?"

Oops.

Bob isn't even trying to act like a chicken. He sticks out one long green finger and points. Then he starts to screech.

Or I thought he was screeching, at first. After a while I figure out that he's actually talking. He's saying, "Meeeeeee! Meeeeeeeee!"

And he's touching the picture on the page. It's definitely a picture of *Bob*.

Same green head.

Same green arms.

Same green body.

Same crooked smile.

Standing right next to a well. It's not this *exact* well. But it's not that different, either.

"Bob!" I shout. "That's YOU. Maybe this well is a passageway. Maybe it leads to your home."

Danny's mouth is hanging open. He says, "A chicken in a *well*?"

Bob breaks into a smile and starts jumping up and down. He turns and actually tries to hug the well. "Oh, Livy! Do you think so? Do you really—"

He stops. He freezes.

I freeze.

Danny freezes.

Because there is a kind of rumbling coming from inside the well.

"What's that noise?" Danny whispers. Before I know it, he's standing behind me, peeking out from under my arm, at the well. "It's *talking*," Danny says into my side.

"It's all right," I tell him. I don't want Danny to get scared. But it doesn't feel completely all right. The well *is* talking. Not in a voice. It's talking with the ground. It's talking with the rocks. It's talking with the trees. It's talking with the birds and the bugs.

It isn't using any words. But with the rocks, and the ground, and the trees, and the birds and the bugs, the well is asking a question:

???

???

???

And then everything starts to move. Still holding the book, I squish Danny against me with one arm and grab Bob's hand on the other side. It feels soft and dry.

And—strong. He's squeezing my hand pretty hard.

We're all looking at the well. More vibrating earth. More shouting trees and birds and bugs.

????

I'm scared. Is the whole town shaking? And right then I have the weirdest thought: Where is my baby sister? Is she safe? I remember she's far away, with Mom. Safe somewhere.

The well wall begins to shake. Danny's arms

go around my waist. And then Bob lets my hand go and takes a step toward the well. "Bob!" I yell, reaching for him. "What are you doing? You've got to hold on to something!"

Bob staggers toward the well, first one foot, then the other. He holds his arms up in the air. It's like when the baby wants *up*.

Something starts coming out of the well. An arm, green like Bob's, but bigger. And then another one.

"Livy!" Bob shouts. "Livy, it's my—"

Then something is in front of us, blotting out the afternoon light. Some*one*.

Someone whose green skin looks wet. Someone whose eyes are just barely open. Like it has been sleeping for a long time. Or crying.

The ground stops shaking. Which is better.

Then the someone puts both arms out, and Bob leaps into them.

"It's my MOM!" Bob shouts at me from her arms. "My MOM, Livy!"

She cuddles Bob up to her face, and he puts his arms around her neck.

Danny lets go of me. "Oh no you don't!" I catch his hand. He pulls, reaching for the little box on the ground. Then, with his free hand, he holds the box up to Bob and his mom.

"Oh, thank you!" Bob says, plucking the cupcake from the box. "Pink!"

"It's for HER," Danny says. "It's a present. She has to take it. So that it can rain again."

But Bob is already eating the cupcake.

"I made it for her! So that we can keep the farm!" Danny says, starting to cry. He turns to me, and his face is crumpled. "Like in the story."

I haven't had a chance to actually read the story, but I already know that Bob's mom doesn't care about cupcakes. Bob's mom cares about Bob.

She puts Bob down very carefully and comes over to me, peering down into my face. (Bob stays put, still eating the cupcake.) She's like a very tall version of Bob, but wet and earth-smelling.

"Hello," I tell her, pretending my legs aren't shaking. "I'm very happy to meet you."

She looks like she's waiting for something. Maybe she *does* want a cupcake. I mean, Bob sure loves them.

"I'm sorry," I say. "I don't have any cupcakes."

She bends toward me, waiting.

"I don't know what you . . ." Then I have an idea. I begin to pull everything out of my pockets. "All I have is *this*." And I hold my hands out, palms up, showing her.

One plastic whistle.

One ripped granola bar wrapper.

One five-year-old piece of licorice.

One black pawn.

I look over at Bob, who's still smacking away. How can he eat at a time like this?

"Livy!" he says between bites. "I am remembering so many things! This is my mother! And this is my well! We have *many* wells. And they are *everywhere*!" Then he pauses, cupcake gripped tightly, pink icing all over his nose, and says, "*Livy*. We are *important*."

"Bob," I say, "could you maybe tell your mom that I don't have any cupcakes?" Because she's staring at me like I have *something* she wants.

"She doesn't want a cupcake!" Bob says, smiling. "She is saying thank you, Livy—she is thanking you for keeping me safe, and for bringing me home."

Then he makes a sound. It's a sound I have never heard from Bob before, not so different from a magpie's warble.

Still looking at me, she makes the same sound.

He makes the sound again. Then he looks sad. "My mom has been waiting for me for a long time, Livy. She says she has missed me even more than I missed her. I have had you, Livy. And Gran Nicholas. And my dictionary. And my Lego pirates. But she missed me very much."

My hands are still out in front of me with all the things from my pockets because I'm afraid to move. I don't want to be afraid of Bob's mom, but I am.

"Give her the licorice!" Danny whispers from behind me.

Bob's mom opens her eyes wide, and I see that they are brown, just like Bob's. They're all *kinds* of brown, like a tree trunk. I stretch out my open hand so that she can take the licorice. Finally, she reaches out with two long fingers. But she doesn't take the licorice. She takes my black pawn.

Her fingers wrap around it, and I can't see it anymore.

Bob's mom makes a light sound, like wind

in the trees, almost a kind of sigh, and then she turns away. She grabs Bob so that he's resting in the crook of one arm. She steps up to the well wall.

Wait. She's not taking him home *right now*, is she? They're just—going away? Is Bob about to disappear? I've been so worried about finding Bob's family that I never for even one second thought about what it would feel like when he left.

It feels horrible.

"Wait!" I yell at Bob's mom's back. "Wait a minute! We didn't get to—"

And she hops into the well.

"Good-bye, Livy!" Bob calls, his words echoing up to us. "Good-bye, my friend! Thank you! I love you, Livy!"

They're gone.

I want to tell Bob that I love him, too.

Everything gets very quiet. And then there's a great big *boom*.

"Thunder!" Danny is jumping up and down, shouting. "Thunder! Finally!" He stops and looks at me. "Everything's going to be okay now!"

Fat, warm raindrops begin falling all around us.

"We did it!" Danny shouts.

The rain is falling heavy and fast. It feels like the air is mostly water. And then, somehow, it rains even harder.

I stand there and let it soak me.

Danny laughs. "You're really wet!" Then he looks serious and says, "But I'm sorry about your chicken."

My Bob. I feel tears start, and I let them come. The rain will hide them.

"We've got to get you home," I tell Danny.

Danny and I have been walking back along the creek bed for less than a minute when two long whistles pierce the sound of the downpour.

Gran! I blow my whistle back to let her know that I'm okay. Danny and I don't try to talk as we make our way to her through the trees. I pay attention to where I walk, the way Gran taught me. It takes me a while to realize I'm squeezing something in one hand. I uncurl my fingers.

One ripped granola bar wrapper.

One piece of licorice.

One plastic whistle.

Wasn't there—something else?

"What was—the other thing?" I shout to Danny through the rain, holding out my hand to show him.

"What?" he shouts back.

"The other thing in my pocket. The thing she took."

"The thing *who* took? Who's *she*?"

I hesitate. I don't know.

"The thing I *lost*." Because I think I lost something. "The black—*something*."

He stops. "Should we look for it?" Danny is a good kid. Maybe Beth Ann will turn out like him.

But the rain is pounding everything. Whatever it was, I know we'll never find it. And anyway, I don't even know what to look for.

CHAPTER TWENTY

BOB

I am home. My home is smelly, wet, and dark. It is also cozy and warm and perfect, and now that I'm back, I remember all the parts of my story.

My mom is here, and my dad, and my two older sisters—Beth and Ann. And lots of grandparents and cousins! We well dwellers don't live inside the actual wells, more like in between them, in long tunnels and caves with nooks and crannies for playing or resting or thinking. We are tied to the earth and the sky, and even though sometimes people bring us treats, they really don't have to. We would bring the rain anyway. It's what we do.

Except when one of us goes missing. This almost never happens, because we are never supposed to leave the wells.

Like, *ever*.

What happens when one of us gets too close to the surface of a well because we smell cake and then hear a small *plop*, followed by a big *plop*?

I. As soon as we climb out and dry off, we forget where we came from, forget how to make rain, and forget how to get home.

2. Our families can't find us and get very, very sad. Our underground tunnels go everywhere, which means that we could pop up anywhere. Well, anywhere there are wells. My mom searched for me in

Istanbul and Singapore, in Finland, Tokyo, and all thirty-eight Springfields in America. She couldn't go far from the wells, though, because of the drying/forgetting thing. She would never have found me in Gran's closet.

3. Without rain, the land soon dries out, the crops don't grow, the animals don't have anything to graze on, the reservoirs don't get filled, and farmers like Gran and her neighbors can't pay their bills anymore.

Basically, it stinks all around.

BUT, once you return to the well, your family is so overjoyed to see you again that they make it pour down rain. In a few days, water will fill the creeks and reservoirs, and rainbows will fill the skies. The grass will get green and the animals will eat and farmers will grow crops again and life will be grand.

Life is grand below, too, because I am exactly where I'm supposed to be. Except—and this is a big one—EXCEPT I've left behind a very smart and brave friend who doesn't remember all the smart and brave things she did because someone's mom (okay, mine) acted all scary and took her pawn away. I don't know how my mom knew that the pawn was the key to Livy remembering me, but she did.

Mom's not *really* scary, not with me anyway. After she found me she told me a story. She said when she'd been looking for me at the Tokyo well, she'd overheard a man telling his son about waku waku, another word that won't be in the *W*s in my Australian/English dictionary.

She said waku waku is a way of describing the thrill you feel at moving toward something that you're excited about, something that makes you feel the most alive out of anything. She said she knew exactly what the man meant, but didn't have a word for it—waku waku is what kept her moving toward me, until I finally got close enough to a well that she found me. Leaning against Gran's well that time with Danny was like a beacon drawing her closer, then touching the old well with the wonky tree led her right to me.

Being a well dweller, and having a friend like Livy, are what make me feel most alive. I can feel the rightness of it all the way to my bones. Now I just need to tell *her*.

So I wait until the middle of the night. I draw my family a picture showing them that I will return soon so they won't worry. Then I put my chicken suit on and hoist a bucketful of water onto my shoulder. When I get back, I will teach my family how to read, so they can learn about things like buckets and I can leave notes with real words. I'm a pretty bad artist.

I climb out of the well and have to climb right back in because it turns out all wells look the same from below. It takes me six tries to find Livy's yard, but I did get to see some cool parts of the world. I'll have to make sure to return to that Hawaii place soon. It looked very green.

Seems I didn't have to worry about keeping myself wet, because the sky over Gran's farm is still pouring down rain. I let the rain soak me through and through, then pour out the bucket and take it with me anyway.

I am so excited as I near the house that I don't even bother with the chicken walk. The smell of freshly baked cake hits me as I slowly push open the back door. It takes supreme willpower to walk by the half-eaten chocolate deliciousness as I pass by it.

On second thought, they probably wouldn't miss a bite or two. I put down the fork after four. I should probably work on this willpower issue.

The lights are out, but I can hear Gran on the phone in her room. She is laughing and saying, "I know, isn't it wonderful? I love the *ping-ping-ping* on the roof. I could listen to it all night. In fact, I plan to!" I put my hand on the wall outside her room and send a silent thank-you for housing me all those years.

Then I pass her half-open door without a sound and enter Livy's bedroom. My feet pull me toward the closet, and I have to remind my-self that it's no longer where I belong. But then I go anyway. I stick the Lego pirate ship and my dictionary and the tutu in the bucket.

The dictionary is to share with everyone. The tutu is for my sisters. The pirate ship is for me. It reminds me of what Livy said, about how one thing can be lots of other things. All it takes is a little imagination.

Now I know that people are like that, too. Livy's not just Old Livy or New Livy, she's every age she's ever been, and sometimes they get jumbled, but they're all in there. All the Bobs are in me, too. All the things I choose to put in my head are what make me, me. I plan to choose wisely.

I am much smarter since I've returned to the wells!

I turn toward Livy now, sleeping soundly with Rufus in her arms. It's the only time I've seen her pay any real attention to him on this trip.

I try not to laugh at the dab of blue paint still on her nose. She also has a smear of chocolate on her cheek. Who needs a bath now!

Then I notice something sticking out from under her pillow. It's the corner of a book. I can read only a little bit of the title—*to Z*—but I know exactly what it is. It's the book with my story in it.

I want to wake her and ask her about it. I want to play chess and solve more mysteries with her. I want to thank her. She protected me, the way a pawn protects the king. Livy got me across the board, and all the way home.

But I let her sleep. I only lift Rufus carefully from her grasp and place the chipped pawn inside the pocket of his tiny overalls. It fits perfectly. Mom had wrapped it up in a cloth and stuck it in a drawer, but I took it out and put a rock in there instead. I learned that from Livy's trick with the pillows in her bed! I hope it will be many years before Mom realizes my deception.

I pat Rufus on the head one last time. It might not work. Maybe Livy will leave him with Gran and won't ever find the pawn. But I hope Livy finds it, and I hope she takes it when she goes back to the other side of the world.

"Keep moving toward what makes you feel most alive, Livy," I whisper. "See you in five years." I tiptoe back to the door, but then remember something really important and tiptoe back to whisper one last thing.

"Bring licorice."

MY FAVORITE WORDS*

BY BOB

*I have many more favorites, but I have to make this quick because my sisters keep tickling me and making me laugh so that my pencil goes all the way across the page. That's sisters for you. But it's important to think about words. You can't understand how you feel sometimes until you know the words for it. Words make things real. You can quote me on that.

BRUNCH [rhymes with LUNCH]: A late-morning meal eaten instead of breakfast and lunch.

I can't believe Livy never told me about brunch. It's half breakfast, half lunch! This word isn't in Gran's old dictionary like the rest of these. My mom "collected it" for me in New York City. Mom and I both love collecting words, and she knows how much I love food. (Mom doesn't like food, but I've told my sisters all about potato chips and beans. Beth likes the idea of potato chips, and Ann likes the idea of beans. I like both, of course. And pancakes.)

ETERNITY [sounds like it-URN-it-ee]: Infinite time without beginning or end.

Time is tricky. The days are long, but the years are short. There are 525,600 minutes in a year, but just *one* minute can feel like an eternity if you're waiting to see someone you love. Or it can feel really short if you need to get all the way across the world because a seven-year-old boy is getting ready to go fishing with his grandpa in a pond that's almost out of water.

He's all pointy elbows and knees and high hopes, and you definitely don't want to disappoint him.

Time is even trickier for well-dwellers because we age reeeeeaaaalllly slowly. Dad said this is why I only grew a millimeter while I was at Gran's house all those years. That's okay. I'm not in any rush to be grown up. From what I can tell, it's not nearly as much fun.

SOLO [sounds like SO-low]: For or done by one person alone; unaccompanied.

Don't get me wrong, I love being with my family. I love exploring every corner of the world together, even if we are mostly exploring underground. I love making rain together and helping nature grow. I love learning new languages together. And I love piling into our great big reading nook with a big stack of books when we have some free time. (Ann loves graphic novels. Beth loves true stories. Mom loves mysteries. Dad's more of a comic-book guy.) But sometimes, believe it or not, I miss my closet. Sometimes, I miss being alone. Something inside me calls out, telling me I need another solo mission.

Usually it's just a walk, an hour of visiting with myself, thinking about my memories, planning my next Lego project, or telling myself all about the things I want to do someday. (One thing is: I really want to try something called soup dumplings. I hope someone drops one near a well soon. Hint, hint.) I don't know whether this is something I had to learn by being at Gran's, or if it's just the way I am. But I love my Bob time.

LIBRARY [sounds like LIE-brare-ee]: A public place containing books that may be read or borrowed.

After I got home, my parents didn't let me leave the well by myself for a long time. (My first solo mission to bring Livy the pawn has remained my secret.) But once they finally tried my water-bucket trick themselves, they couldn't wait to pop out of every well. EVERY well. That's how we discovered our first library.

Just the word *library* sends shivers of anticipation through me. I thought at first it was a made-up place, but no, libraries are real! They actually LEND YOU BOOKS FOR FREE! Well, not to me because they don't let fake chickens get library cards, but, if there are no kids around, I can walk right in and none of the grown-ups see me. I read over their shoulders sometimes, but mostly I just run my hands along the spines as I walk the stacks and marvel at all the stories and knowledge tucked away inside the books.

Once, I poked my head out of a well in Reykjavik, Iceland, to see if it's true that Greenland is icy and Iceland is green (it is! and also, it's *hot* underground there!) and guess what

I found in the middle of a park? A wooden box stuck on a pole labeled *Little Free Library*! The books are free, and you get to keep them! I've now discovered these boxes ALL OVER THE WORLD! This is how we filled the book nook Dad dug for me after I first came home. Anytime I leave the wells, I bring books to fill the boxes so people who don't have books can find them. Beth made me my own library card, and I carry it everywhere. One day I'll figure out a way to get into a bookstore, too. Then I can buy my own copy of *Fairy and Folk Tales from A to Z*. But that one I'm going to keep.

URANUS [sounds like YOOR-in-us *or* yoo-RAY-nuhs]: The seventh planet from the sun.

How could you not love a word that you can pronounce two ways and both ways make you giggle? Maybe the person who named it lost a truth or dare game and the dare was they had to give it the weirdest name they could think of. Uranus is the third largest planet in our solar system, and the coldest. With the help of one of my new books (and my excellent eyesight) I was able to find it in the night sky last week! I couldn't see any of its impressive twenty-seven moons, though. Wouldn't it be awesome to be on Uranus and look up at the sky and see all those moons just hanging there? Makes our one moon seem pretty boring.

Speaking of weird names for things, I recently asked my parents why they named me Bob. They said they liked that it could be said backward or forward and still sound the same. I showed them the word *palindrome* in the dictionary, and now they want to turn Ann's name into *Anna,* but she insists that she's happy with her name as it is, thank you very much. Beth, however, has changed her full name to Bethteb. We still call her Beth.

DELUGE [sounds like day-LOOJ]: A sudden large amount of rain (also refers to flooding or an inundation of anything).

When we need to deliver a *lot* of water in a very short time, we create a deluge. It's not as easy as it sounds. Mom can make one herself, and Beth can *almost* do it, but Ann and I have to hold hands. Gran's town didn't turn green again until there were a whole bunch of deluges, plus a lot of regular-type rain. I like thinking that the same rain that falls on the farm once fell on the dinosaurs, then sank into the earth, then evaporated, then came back down again. Over and over. (I wonder if it rains on Uranus?) I like looking at Gran's horses, which finally came back, too, when the grass grew again.

Once, during a drizzle, I was sitting on the Sylvester rock, watching the horses, when I saw someone crossing the yard to Gran's door. It took me a while to realize it was Danny. Danny got tall! I waved, but he couldn't see me. Maybe he got too old. He was smiling, though, just walking in the rain. I made it rain a little harder, and he laughed. I guess Danny will love the rain forever.

SERENDIPITY [sounds like SER-in-dip-it-ee]: The occurrence of an event by chance in a happy or beneficial way. A happy accident.

How could I not love this word? Serendipity is what brought me to Livy, and Livy to me.

What could be a happier accident than me and Livy inside the same small well, inside the same small town, at the exact same time? I think we both saved each other after all. My life is so much fuller than before I met her, in ways it would take me another five years to count.

Plus, serendipity sounds a little like the name of a dessert, don't you think? If I could invent a cookie, this is what I would name it. The serendipity cookie would have caramel

(Livy's favorite) and licorice (my favorite). And chocolate. Of course.

Ann is threatening to put on my tutu if I don't stop writing now, and I've grown very attached to that tutu, so I'd better go play with them. I'm going to save this notebook to show Livy one day. And with time being the trickster that it is, I know I'll see her soon. Well, soon-ish.

Okay, this is Bob, over and out.

GOFISH

WENDY MASS AND REBECCA STEAD

How did you decide to write a book together?
When we met, we'd already read and admired each other's books and thought we had a lot in common in terms of how we see the world. It took us a while to find the right story, but after *seven years* of passing chapters back and forth, we had a book!

How did you create each of the main characters, Bob and Livy?
Rebecca wrote the first chapter on a long flight home from Australia, not really knowing who these characters would turn out to be. The chapter ended with the introduction of Bob, who had been waiting in his closet for five years. That first chapter was from Livy's point of view, so when Wendy wrote the next chapter, she naturally became Bob. The characters grew as we wrote and became more real as we got to know them.

What was the most fun about writing *Bob* together?
It was fun having a secret project that only our families knew about. We were very patient and kind with each

other, not nagging if a chapter was left dangling for eight months while we wrote our other books, raised families, got waylaid by the stuff of life. It was really lovely to have a partnership based on trust, respect, admiration, and the ability to make each other laugh along the way.

What was the biggest challenge about writing *Bob* together?

Wendy is a plotter, writing thorough outlines before she begins a book. Rebecca likes to let a story grow organically, not sure what will happen next. In the end we met each other halfway—and both learned things that we'll take back into writing our own books.

What did you want to be when you grew up?

Wendy wanted to be an astronaut, but her parents gently reminded her that she gets carsick in the back seat of a car, so soaring around space in zero gravity probably wasn't her best career option. But now she gets to write about outer space, so it's a win-win! Rebecca wanted to be an actress or a veterinarian.

Where do you write your books?

Anywhere and anytime! Sometimes on paper, sometimes on the computer, often in our heads. If your teacher catches you daydreaming in class, you can tell them you're writing a story in your head! But don't say you heard that from us ;o)

Bob loves the dictionary. What is *your* favorite word?
Wendy: *Magic.*
Rebecca: *Wonderful.*

What was your favorite book when you were a kid?
Wendy: The Chronicles of Narnia series and books by Edward Eager, Ray Bradbury, and Judy Blume.

Rebecca: I loved *To Kill a Mockingbird* by Harper Lee, *I Know Why the Caged Bird Sings* by Maya Angelou, and *Red Planet* by Robert A. Heinlein.

What do you want readers to remember about *Bob*?
That true friendships help you see the best parts of yourself. We miss Livy and Bob, but we know they're out there in the world, tucked safely away in readers' minds and hearts. That means everything to us.